MONSTER BLOOD
IS BACK

GOOSEBUMPS®

Also available as ebooks

ALSO AVAILABLE:

MONSTER BLOOD IS BACK

R.L. STINE

SCHOLASTIC INC.

Goosebumps book series created by Parachute Press, Inc.
Copyright © 2021 by Scholastic Inc.

ISBN 978-1-338-35579-6

10 9 8 7 6 5 4 3 2 1   21 22 23 24 25

Printed in the U.S.A.   40
First printing 2021

SLAPPY HERE, EVERYONE.

Welcome to *SlappyWorld*.

Yes, it's Slappy's world—you're only *screaming* in it! Hahahaha!

I know you're glad to see me. I'm always glad to see me! I'm so awesome, I want to turn my mouth around and kiss myself! (But I don't want to get splinters! Hahahaha.)

Am I good-looking? You don't have to answer. I know you're too busy admiring me!

I'm so handsome, when I look in a mirror, the mirror says, *"Thank you!"* Hahaha.

Do you know the only thing that's almost as good-looking as my face? A *photo* of my face! Haha.

Why do people invite me to so many parties? Because I'm a *scream*!

Bet I can make *you* scream. Know what I'm cooking up?

A story about a TV cooking competition. It's about a girl named Sascha and her friend Nicole.

1

They have a can of something disgusting—a can of *Monster Blood*.

What happens when the Monster Blood becomes an ingredient in their dish? That's a good recipe—a recipe for *horror*! Hahaha.

I know you're hungry for thrills. Go ahead and start reading.

It's another one of my tasty tales from *SlappyWorld*!

On the day my friend Nicole and I found the Monster Blood and totally ruined our lives, we were both excited and happy enough to burst.

That's because we had a chance to be on our favorite TV series.

A chance to show off the cooking skills we had practiced in my kitchen. All the crazy dishes Nicole and I dreamed up. Slapping food together in the craziest combinations. Dreaming up wild new desserts and pasta casseroles and soups and stews that sometimes even *we* were afraid to taste!

Before I go too far, let me say that I'm Sascha Nelson. My best friend, Nicole Hilliard, and I are twelve, and we consider ourselves kitchen explorers. *We go where no chefs have ever gone before.*

No joke.

I mean, who else would think of making salty chocolate milk? Or scrambled eggs with Marshmallow Fluff? Or a bologna cake?

We're pioneers. We're inventors. We're creators. We're totally nuts.

At least, that's what my mom and dad say. But what do *they* know? They put jelly on their peanut butter instead of bananas and pickles!

Who could compete against us in the kitchen?

We were about to find out. Because—wait for this—Nicole and I were picked for the most awesome TV cooking show in the universe.

Unless you're new to this planet, you know what I'm talking about. *Kids' Big Chef Food Fights.*

That's the one. Three teams of kids competing for the Silver Spatula. That spatula is worth two thousand dollars!

Can you get excited about two thousand dollars? Nicole and I sure could.

All the contestants were coming from our school, Adam Driver Middle School. Nicole and I knew we could out-cook anyone in school with our oven mitts tied behind our backs.

Sure. Maybe I brag a lot. But if you've got something to brag about, why not?

After school on Thursday, we couldn't wait to get to the TV studio. Luckily, it was only a six-block walk from my house. Nicole and I were in my kitchen, loosening up.

"Let's make an ice cream sundae," I said. "Put everything we can find on it."

Nicole nodded. "Yeah. We need to carb up,

you know." She flexed her arm muscles. "Get the energy flowing."

"Mainly I just want a sundae," I said.

We pulled a carton of vanilla ice cream from the freezer. I found chopped walnuts and caramel syrup and colored sprinkles in the pantry. Nicole produced a banana from the fridge. "Do you have any popcorn?" she asked. "I love popcorn on ice cream."

"I don't think so," I said. "There's a bag of tortilla chips. We could crumble some chips on it."

I found a tall can of whipped cream in the refrigerator door. You know, the whipped cream with a nozzle that you push and it sprays out.

"This is a good start," I said. "We can build the sundae, then see what else we can find."

Nicole glanced at the clock above the kitchen window. "It's getting late. Maybe we should just have some ice cream."

"No way," I insisted. "This is going to be an awesome creation."

I pulled a glass ice cream dish from the cabinet and started to scoop ice cream into it. Nicole heated the caramel sauce in the microwave. Then she poured it on top of the ice cream scoops.

We were adding the banana slices when Toby came bursting into the kitchen.

Toby is my little brother. He's eight going on four. What I mean is, he's a pain.

It's hard to get mad at him because he looks so

much like me. Bouncy red hair, a round face with freckled cheeks. But I have blue eyes and his are brown.

"Hey, Toby." I followed his gaze. Guessed what he was about to do—but I was too slow to stop him.

He grabbed the can of whipped cream off the counter and raised it high, aiming it at me.

"Toby, put that down," I said. "I mean it."

He moved his finger to the top, ready to press it. He giggled. He has a seriously evil giggle. "Tell me what you got me for my birthday," he said.

"Put it down," I said.

"I'll put it down when you tell me my birthday present." He pointed the can at my face.

"I'm not telling," I said.

I *couldn't* tell him, because I hadn't bought him anything yet. Who wants to shop for an eight-year-old pest?

He giggled again. Then he pressed the nozzle and shot a big blob of whipped cream into my face.

"Hey—!" I let out a shout. I wiped the stuff from my eyes with one hand—and grabbed for the can with my other hand. Missed.

He sprayed another white stream at me. I ducked and it sailed over my shoulder and splattered the stove.

"Give me that!" I screamed. I swiped at the can, but he pulled it away. And sent a big wet blob of whipped cream onto my shoes.

6

"I've got him!" Nicole cried. She grabbed Toby from behind and tried to pin his arms back.

Laughing, he sprayed her face and hair with whipped cream. A thick white stripe of it spread along the side of the kitchen counter. He shot a big circle of the cream onto the wall.

"Give it! Give it, you jerk!" I screamed, grabbing wildly for the can.

That's when I saw Mom and Dad standing in the doorway.

Toby must have seen them, too, because he tossed the whipped cream can into my hands.

Nicole was too busy trying to wipe the stuff from her hair to notice them. Big splotches of whipped cream covered the floor and the kitchen cabinets.

Mom pressed her hands to the sides of her face. "What on earth is going on here?" she cried.

"Sascha and Nicole were having a whipped cream fight," Toby said.

2

"Your little brother needs to be taught a lesson," Nicole said.

"What lesson?" I asked.

"That he is obnoxious," she said.

I laughed. "Is that a lesson?"

It was fifteen minutes later. Nicole and I had done our best to wipe the whipped cream off everything. And then we listened to a lecture from my dad about how we had to take better care of Toby when we were in charge.

We didn't think we were in charge. But we listened anyway because we were eager to get out of the house.

Now the afternoon sun was sliding behind the trees, and long shadows stretched across the front lawns. We crossed the street and made our way toward the TV studio, taking long strides.

Nicole kept tugging at her hair. A big clump of it was stuck together because of the whipped cream.

"There won't be any cameras. This is just a tryout," I told her.

But that didn't make her feel any better.

Nicole has beautiful long straight black hair. Sometimes she ties it in a single braid. But today it fell behind her back like a dark waterfall.

We walked past our school. Five or six kids had a soccer game going on at the playground. Some girls from the elementary school had dropped their bikes on the front lawn and were sprawled on the grass, hanging out.

"I wonder what kind of ingredients we'll get for the tryout," I said. My stomach felt a little fluttery. You can't blame me for feeling a little tense.

"Probably octopus and pine nuts," Nicole joked.

See, the way the contest works is this: Every team gets a box with the same bunch of ingredients in it. No one knows what's inside until you open the box. Then you have to make something delicious from the ingredients.

Something more delicious than the other two teams have made.

A few weekends ago, Nicole and I did a practice session. We asked my mom to pull four ingredients out for us. We closed our eyes while she scurried around the kitchen.

When we opened our eyes, we saw her four ingredients on the counter. A box of macaroni noodles. Two apples. A jar of honey. And a little spice jar of cinnamon.

Nicole and I studied them for a while. Then we mixed everything together and baked the whole thing. And it came out as a very sweet pasta dessert.

Has anyone ever cooked a pasta dessert before? Maybe Nicole and I invented something new!

I was thinking about that dessert when the car came squealing around the corner.

I didn't realize it was a car at first. I just saw a whirring blur of black.

I heard the car's engine roar. The tires squealed. And then it came into focus as it wheeled around the corner. A long black SUV.

"Sascha—look out!"

I heard Nicole's scream.

I leaped backward. Fell hard onto my back. My head smacked the pavement with a *thud*. The breath whooshed from my chest.

I'm hit! I told myself. *I'm hit! I'm hit! That car ... it hit me!*

My head throbbed. I saw red.

I shut my eyes tight ... and waited for the pain to fade.

3

I opened my eyes to see Nicole's face close above mine. She knelt down beside me. Her hands cradled my head, lifting it from the curb.

Her violet eyes were wide with horror, and her chin trembled as she stared at me.

The throbbing pain at the back of my head faded to a low ache. I blinked a few times. "I think I'm okay." My voice came out in a whisper.

"He just kept driving," Nicole said, gazing down the street. "He didn't stop."

She helped raise me to a sitting position. I rubbed the back of my head. "Must have hit my head when I fell."

She squinted at me. "Are you okay? Should I call 911?"

I shook my head hard, trying to clear it. "I'm okay." With a groan, I stood up. Shook my head again. "Yeah. I'm all right," I said. "I'm not even dizzy."

I bent my knees. Checked out my jeans. My

T-shirt. "He missed me by inches," I said. "If I hadn't jumped back . . ." My voice trailed off.

Nicole searched her backpack. "I couldn't call 911 even if we needed to," she said. "I left my phone at school."

"We don't need it," I said. "Come on. Let's hurry."

We started walking again. A school bus whirred past, and it made me jump.

Guess what? I still didn't feel normal. If a car nearly runs you down, it kind of shakes you up.

We crossed Harrison Street and turned onto Jackson. The late-afternoon sunlight made my head throb. I kept shielding my eyes with one hand.

"Hey, look." Nicole pointed. "I don't remember seeing that store before."

I squinted across the street. "Must be new," I said. "We've walked here a million times, and I never saw it before, either."

As we came closer, I saw toys and games in the front window. "Let's go in, Sascha," Nicole said. "Maybe you should sit down for a few minutes. You still look kinda shaky."

"Okay," I said. I wanted to get the sun out of my eyes.

"Maybe we can find a birthday present for Toby here," Nicole said.

We stepped under the awning. A black-and-purple sign above the door read VERY EVIL TOYS.

Strange name, huh?

Maybe we should have taken the hint—and beat it. Maybe we should have hurried away from there as fast as we could.

But Nicole and I were curious, so we went in.

And that's when all the trouble started.

I followed Nicole into the store. And waited for my eyes to adjust to the sudden darkness. Tiny red ceiling lights spread a dim glow over the narrow room.

"Spooky," I whispered.

And then the man behind the counter came into focus. He wore a black robe, his face hidden beneath its dark hood. He stared at a newspaper on the counter.

I gazed down a long, cluttered aisle. It had boxes stacked high and stuffed creatures scattered all over the floor. Some were sitting. Some were standing. All in positions that made them look strangely alive. At the end of the aisle was a display case bursting with toys and gadgets.

"Sascha, I don't believe this place," Nicole whispered.

Then the hooded man behind the counter finally raised his eyes to us. And I could see his face. *No face*. No face at all. Just a pale skull reflecting the glare of the dim red lights.

I screamed. I couldn't help myself.

And he laughed. A dry laugh, kind of like crackling dead leaves.

He lifted a hand and pulled off the skull. A mask. He was wearing a skull mask.

He grinned at us. He had wide dark eyes and a black mustache on a pale round face. His bald head glowed in the dim light. "Did I frighten you?" His voice was soft, almost a whisper.

"A little," I said.

He laughed. "It's Halloween all year round in my store," he said. "Welcome. My name is Bardo."

Nicole and I stepped closer to the counter. "It's so dark in here," I said.

He nodded. "I live in darkness."

"Is this store new?" Nicole asked.

A thin smile spread across his pale face. "It's new and it's old." Bardo tapped his fingers on the glass countertop. He had long, pointed finger-nails painted black. "What kind of evil toys are you ladies looking for?" he asked.

My throat was suddenly dry. My headache was a dull pain at the back of my neck. The store was creeping me out. And I could see that Nicole felt the same way.

Why didn't we leave when we had a chance?

"I need something for my little brother," I said. "He's eight."

"That's a frightening age," Bardo said. He grinned. "But I have the perfect thing."

15

He reached under the counter and pulled up a large box. "Boys really love this," he said, tapping his long nails on it. "It's a cockroach farm."

"A *what*?" Nicole and I both blurted out at once.

"A cockroach farm," he repeated. He turned the box so we could see the front. "See? You hatch the cockroaches in this container. And then they live in this glass case. Plenty of room for them to run around."

"But—but—" I sputtered.

Bardo smiled that thin smile. "You just have to be careful to keep the lid on," he said.

I shook my head. "I don't think so," I said.

He nodded. He lowered the box to the bottom shelf. Then he raised another box. I could see a plastic white-and-yellow flower in it that looked like a daisy.

"Perfect for an eight-year-old," Bardo said. "You wear it on your T-shirt. It's a squirting flower. Very special."

I squinted at it. "What's special about it?"

"It shoots black ink pellets," he replied, waving the box in front of me. "The color never comes off. It's totally permanent."

"No way," I said. "My parents would kill me."

"Okay, okay," he said. "I have lots of evil toys for an eight-year-old. Follow me."

He stepped around the counter and crossed to the nearest display case. He scratched his bald head, then pulled something from the case. "How about this cat?"

He shoved it in front of my face. A gray-and-white stuffed cat, actual cat size.

"I think Toby is too old for a stuffed animal," I said.

He smiled and shook his head. When he smiled, his black mustache slid up with his mouth. "You don't understand. Here. Hold out your hand."

I stuck my right hand out.

He squeezed the cat's tail—and the cat *bit* me!

"Ouch!" I let out a cry as the hard cat teeth clamped onto the back of my hand.

Nicole gasped. "A stuffed animal that *bites*?"

Bardo nodded, grinning. "Boys love it." He squeezed the tail again and the teeth lifted off my hand. It's from a company called Gruff Pets."

The back of my hand had teeth marks. I tried to rub the pain away. "No!" I told Bardo. "Definitely not! My brother is already a total menace!"

He sighed and looked very disappointed.

"We only have a few minutes," Nicole told him. "Why don't Sascha and I wander around on our own?"

We walked to the back of the store.

"I see why he calls this store 'Very Evil Toys,'" Nicole whispered, tossing back her long black hair.

"Toby would *love* everything in here," I whispered. "And then he'd torture us all forever."

17

"Sascha, are you feeling better?" she asked. "We should get going."

I didn't answer. I had my eyes on a stack of blue cans on the back shelf. The cans were about the size of soda cans, and they had green labels on one side.

"What's that?" Nicole leaned closer to see them better.

"I don't know." I picked up a can and read the label out loud to her: *"Monster Blood Is Back!"*

"Huh?" Nicole squinted at it. "Monster Blood?"

She took the blue can from me and started to pry the lid off—and the store owner let out a shriek: "NOOOO! DON'T OPEN THAT!"

Bardo's heavy robe brushed the floor as he ran toward us, waving both hands. "Don't open it, girls!" he repeated breathlessly.

Nicole lowered the can in front of her. "What's wrong?"

He rubbed sweat off his bald head. "You have to buy it if you want to open it," he said. "It won't be fresh if the air hits it." He took the can from Nicole's hand.

"Fresh?" I said. "What is Monster Blood? Do you eat it?"

He shook his head. "Eat it? No. It's just green slime. You know. Kids love to play with slime. It's perfectly harmless."

I gazed at the stack of cans. "Toby likes to play with anything that's gross and slimy," I said to Nicole. "He even makes his own slime. It's disgusting."

"Buy him some Monster Blood," Nicole said. "His birthday gift. Done."

I picked up two cans and handed them to Bardo. "I'll take them."

They were only two dollars a can. Cheap. I tucked them into my backpack.

"A pleasure doing business with you," Bardo said. "Any time you need evil toys, you know where to come."

I followed Nicole back outside. The sun had darkened to red. It hung lower in the sky. And the spring air now felt cool against my cheeks.

We started to trot along the sidewalk. The TV studio was two blocks away. We didn't want to be late for our tryout.

A few minutes later, the building came into view. A three-story white granite office building with a neon sign over one door that read GREEN-LIGHT STUDIOS.

My heart started to pound as we stepped inside. A receptionist by the door pointed. "It's Studio B-3," she said. "The kitchen set."

Nicole and I turned and hurried down the hall. Our shoes thundered over the marble floor. I sucked in a deep breath and held it, trying to force away my nervousness.

We stopped outside the glass doors of Studio B-3. Inside, I could see several kitchens set up— stoves and sinks and wall cabinets—in a circle. A lot of people wearing headphones were hurrying around. And one of the little kitchen areas already had kids hanging out inside it. A cooking team waiting to start.

I counted three video cameras inside the circle. And a long wooden table with chairs outside the circle. I guessed that's where the judges sat.

I turned to Nicole. "Are you nervous?" I asked.

She frowned at me. "Does a bear burp in the woods?"

Did I mention she always gets weird when she's stressed out?

"Come on. We're gonna rock this contest!" I said. I grabbed the handle and pulled the door.

It didn't budge.

I pulled harder. No.

I gave the other door a hard tug. It wouldn't move.

I turned to Nicole with a sigh. "We must be too late," I said. "We're locked out."

Nicole laughed. She pointed at the door handle. "It says *push*."

I could feel myself blushing. "Oh, wow. Guess I'm a little nervous, too."

I pushed open the door and we stepped into the studio. We were instantly greeted by the sound of two dozen people talking at once. Over the roar, a man's voice boomed on a loudspeaker: "We can kill the lights, people. We're not recording this, remember?"

That's why the three cameras were standing without anyone behind them. This was just a tryout to see which teams would make it to the actual TV show.

Nicole and I stood awkwardly by the door, watching everyone scamper around. We recognized the kids from our school on the other teams. I called out to my friend Debra. But she was busy talking with Miller, her partner.

A young man came striding toward us, waving

a clipboard at his side. He had short blond hair and blue eyes, and his cheeks were tanned, covered in blond stubble. He wore a dark blue blazer over a white shirt, a red necktie loosely tied, and tight, straight-legged jeans.

"Hello, hello," he said. "Welcome."

"Thank you," Nicole and I said in unison.

"I'm Heston," he said. "Heston Hill. I'm an exec producer. Everyone calls me Hess. And you are . . ." He checked his clipboard. "Sascha and Nicole?"

"That's us," I said.

"Kitchen number two," he said, making check marks on his paper. He pointed. "You know how it works, right?"

"Yeah. We watch the show all the time," I said.

"We cook a lot," Nicole chimed in. "We're really awesome cooks."

Hess stared at her. "I like your self-confidence," he said. "Keep that enthusiasm going."

"No problem," Nicole said.

Where did she get that confidence?

My legs felt like rubber bands as we walked to our kitchen. And my chest was all fluttery, like I had a hummingbird inside it.

"This is cozy," Nicole said. We checked out our counter and the stove and oven. We opened the cabinet. It was filled with spices and ketchup and mustard and stuff to add to our food dishes.

I waved across the counter to Debra, and she

waved back. She mouthed the words *Good luck.* Her partner, Miller, made a face at us.

Then the man's voice on the loudspeaker rose over the huge room again. "Are we ready to begin? The judges are finishing their cocktail hour. They are ten minutes away. Hess, are the teams in place?"

"We are waiting for one more team," Hess said into his mouthpiece. "Oh, wait. Here they come."

The glass doors opened, and a boy and a girl walked into the studio. I recognized them immediately. I gasped and let out a cry: "Oh NO!"

Beside me, Nicole groaned. "Oh, please. Give us a break."

Hess was checking them off on his clipboard. Then he pointed them to the kitchen next to ours.

Ashli Lorraine and Nathan Diggs.

The two biggest cheaters on earth.

The two kids in school who *nobody* likes. Take my word. I'll bet you even their parents can't stand them!

Ashli and Nathan.

Just thinking their names brought back my headache.

"I didn't know they were chosen," I whispered to Nicole.

"Bad news," she muttered.

Ashli and Nathan are stuck-up rich kids. They always seem to be laughing at everyone else. They never really smile. They only smirk.

They always have their own private jokes.

25

And you just know the jokes are making fun of someone.

And did I mention they are both horrible cheaters?

They copy their book reports off ones they find on the internet. And they *brag* about it.

Last month, they knew my papier-mâché lion head was good enough to win the sixth-grade art show. So they sneaked into the art room, poured water on it, and turned it into mush.

I know it was Ashli and Nathan.

Who else would do that?

They both have Apple Watches, and they use them to send each other the answers during math quizzes.

I could go on, but I'm sure you get the idea.

Whenever they get in real trouble, their rich parents swoop in and make sure they don't get punished for it.

"Bad news," Nicole whispered. "They're going to be cooking right next to us."

"Just ignore them," I said. "I'll bet they've never cooked a thing in their lives. Wonder why they're doing this."

"To be on TV," Nicole replied. "To be *stars*."

Ashli had her straw-blond hair tied in a single braid on one side. She wore white tennis shorts and a violet T-shirt that said *Designer T-Shirt* on the front.

Nathan always wears silver-lensed sunglasses

day or night. He has a gold ring in one ear. He wore a black sweatshirt with the sleeves rolled up and a big hole at the collar, and straight-legged black jeans.

They stepped into the kitchen area beside us and dropped their backpacks loudly onto the counter. Then they gazed around the studio.

Since they were right next to us, I had to say hi. "How's it going?" I asked.

Nathan lowered his sunglasses and squinted at me like I was from some other species he'd never seen before. "Yo," he said.

"Hey," Ashli said. She didn't look up. She was searching for something in her backpack.

There was an awkward silence.

"Are you nervous?" Nicole asked them finally.

"Should we be?" Ashli replied with a sneer.

Nathan pulled something from his backpack and slid it onto the shelf at his side. Then he leaned over the low wall between the two kitchens. "Don't get too close to our stove," he said. "Ashli and I get in a zone when we cook, and we can't be held responsible."

Was he threatening us?
What did that even mean?

"The judges are here," the voice on the loud-speaker announced. "Let's get rolling before these kids graduate from college. Hess, where are the boxes of ingredients?"

"They're still in my van," Hess replied. "I sent Morgan and Courtney to carry them in." Morgan and Courtney were Hess's assistants.

Two men and a woman had entered through the glass doors. The contest judges. Hess hurried to greet them.

Ashli was still pawing through her backpack. Nathan got a text on his iPhone and was busy typing a reply. On our other side, Debra and Miller leaned on their counter, not talking, just waiting.

Three teams. Which of us would pass the try-out and go on to the real show?

I looked down. I had my fingers crossed on both hands and didn't even realize it. Nicole had a water bottle tilted to her mouth and drank half of it down.

Nathan finished typing his text and turned back to us. "After Ashli and I win this, we'll probably get our own TV series," he said. "We'll let you know when it's on so you two can watch." He snickered as if he had just made a very funny joke.

"What makes you think Nicole and I are going to lose?" I demanded.

He didn't answer. He just laughed. Then he turned to Ashli and said something to her about ingredients.

I wanted to punch the grin off his face. But I knew that was a bad attitude to start the competition.

Nicole shook her head. "They probably cheated already," she whispered. "They probably found a way to get the list of ingredients in advance."

"It won't help them," I said. "We know we can out-cook them."

I said those bold words to Nicole. But I had a heavy feeling the weight of a large rock in the pit of my stomach. And I suddenly had all kinds of doubts. Like, did we really belong here? What if the other two teams knew what they were doing and were a lot better than us?

I took a deep breath and told myself to stop being stupid. I'm almost always a confident person. But you understand, right? I'd never had to compete for a chance to be on TV—and two thousand dollars—before.

The two young women, Morgan and Courtney, returned to the studio, carrying cardboard boxes. They dropped one on the counter in front of each team.

"Okay, people," Hess shouted into a microphone. "Showtime."

The room grew quiet. Nicole and I turned and flashed thumbs-ups to Debra and Miller. I watched them for a short while. I wanted to see if they were nervous, too.

"As I think you know," Hess said, "this is a one-round tryout. Your one chance to go on to the TV show to try for the Silver Spatula. Only one team will win. That's the team our three judges decide is the most creative and presents the most delicious dish."

The judges sat side by side behind their table. Each of them held an iPad in front of them. I wasn't sure what the iPads were for. All three of them smiled across the room at us and gave us a short wave. I guess they were encouraging us.

I needed to be encouraged. My hands were wet and ice-cold. I rubbed them along the legs of my jeans.

"Okay, teams," Hess shouted. "Open the boxes. Let's see what four ingredients you will all be cooking with!"

A blast of music burst from the loudspeaker. I

guess they wanted to add more excitement and tension.

Nicole and I reached for our box at the same time. And we both lifted the lid. We gazed inside.

And then we both opened our mouths in gasps of horror.

9

The music stopped.

"W-worms!" I choked out.

Nicole and I both stepped back from the open box. Inside it, on top of the ingredients, at least a dozen purple-brown worms crawled over one another in a tangled heap. Like fat spaghetti come to life!

The sour aroma of dirt and worm slime invaded my nose and mouth, and I started to cough. Nicole grabbed my shoulder and squeezed it.

"What's wrong, Team Two?" Hess said, walking slowly toward our kitchen.

"Worms," I repeated, pointing into the box. "It's so gross."

Then I realized that in the kitchen next to us, Ashli and Nathan were laughing. Nathan kept pointing to the box and hee-hawing so hard, he had tears in his eyes.

"You should have seen your faces!" Ashli exclaimed. "Priceless! Priceless!"

Hess leaned over the table, peered into the box,

and grinned. "Did you get those at a bait shop?" he asked Ashli and Nathan. "Wish I was on the lake with my fishing rod. Those are beauties."

"But . . . aren't they going to get in trouble for doing this to us?" I said.

"I like trouble," Hess replied. "It makes for a more exciting show."

Nathan grinned at us. "I slipped them into your box while you two were looking at Debra and Miller," he said.

"Nathan and I like to shake things up," Ashli chimed in.

"People! People!" the voice on the loudspeaker interrupted. "Can we get serious now? We only have the studio for two hours."

On our other side, Debra leaned toward me. "I'd rather eat those worms than what those two are going to cook!" she exclaimed.

Nathan sneered at her. "No one asked you."

Hess shook his head. "We are all here to have fun. Let's be nice to one another, guys."

Morgan dropped a fresh box of ingredients on our counter.

"Can we get started?" the loudspeaker voice said. "Check out your ingredients boxes."

I pictured the fat, slithery worms again. I felt embarrassed that I'd made such a fuss over a bunch of worms. It was babyish. Nicole's cheeks were still red.

Ashli and Nathan knew we were better cooks

than them. They just wanted to shake us up before the contest started.

I tipped open the lid to the new box, and we both peered inside.

I saw three eggs, a bag of mushrooms, a chunk of cheddar cheese, and a slab of Canadian bacon.

"Okay. Ready, everyone?" Hess said. "Let's see who can make the tastiest dish from those four ingredients. You have twenty minutes."

Next to us, I saw Ashli and Nathan grinning at each other. "This is too easy. We've already won," Ashli said, loud enough for everyone to hear.

Nathan saw me watching them. "Hey, Sascha— don't copy us," he said. "We'll turn you in if we see you watching us."

You two are the cheaters, I thought. I spun angrily away from them.

"You can use only the four ingredients from the box," Hess said. "Plus the spices and condiments in the cabinets behind you. Good luck. Get cooking!"

Everyone on the three teams started moving at once.

Nicole rubbed her chin and gazed at the ingredients. "What do you think?"

"I think we can make a perfect omelet from these," I said. I glanced at the big round clock on the far wall. "Twenty minutes is more than enough time."

We were a great team. Nicole and I had cooked together so often. We went into action.

Frying pan out and greased. Eggs broken. Mushrooms and bacon sliced and chopped. Cheese cut into small chunks.

We worked quickly and smoothly as we prepared the ingredients. Then we dropped everything into the frying pan. I set it on the stove at a medium heat.

The omelet began to sizzle, and I lifted it with a spatula to let the runny part flow to the edges of the pan.

Then I glanced around the room.

The other two teams appeared to be a little frantic, everyone talking at once and moving at super-fast speed. They kept opening and closing cabinet doors, mixing ingredients, and slamming frying pans on their stovetop.

"Looking good!" I told Nicole.

I heard a crash. I turned toward it and saw that Miller had dropped a bowl of grated cheese on the floor. He and Debra scurried to clean it up.

Whoa.

A flash of movement made me blink. I spun around. Nathan was leaning over our side of the counter.

"Hey—!" I snapped. "Nathan—what are you doing over here? Did I just see you move near our stove?"

He went wide-eyed. "Huh?

"Did you just pour something into our omelet?" I demanded. "Did I just see you over here?"

"Are you serious?" Nathan cried. "I didn't touch your omelet. I just reached over to borrow your saltshaker." He waved the saltshaker in the air.

I turned to Nicole. She shook her head. "I didn't see anything. I had my eyes on the judges."

"You two are just freaking out because you know you can't win," Ashli chimed in.

Our omelet was finished. I turned off the heat and carried the skillet to the counter.

"It looks awesome," Nicole said. She used a spatula to transfer it to a serving dish. "Smells great, too."

I jumped as a loud buzzer erupted.

"Time's up!" Hess shouted. "Ovens off, everyone! Put down your utensils. It's time to be judged!"

10

Chairs scraped as the three judges moved closer to their table. They shifted papers around and tapped on their iPads, getting ready to judge.

Hess introduced them as Larry Ming-Lee, Mary Franklin, and Jake Fortuna. Larry was an older man, dressed in a dark suit and tie. He had friendly dark eyes and black hair brushed straight back off his forehead.

Mary was about my mom's age. She had her brown hair piled up in a bun with a bandanna tied around it, and wore bright orange lipstick.

Jake was young and very thin. He wore a blue polo shirt over denim jeans. He seemed tense. He kept tapping a pencil on the tabletop.

Nicole and I bumped knuckles for luck. I felt a little fluttery and my hands were suddenly cold and clammy.

It would be so awesome to win this tryout and go on TV, I thought. *Not to mention the two-thousand-dollar prize.*

Hess checked his clipboard, then set it down. "Team Number One," he announced. "Debra and Miller. We'll taste your entry first."

He carried their serving dish to the judges' table. The judges cut slices of it and set them on their plates.

Mary sat between the two men. She sniffed the dish. "Mmm. Smells wonderful. What is this you have made for us?"

"It's a cheese and mushroom pie," Debra answered.

"This is like a quiche," Larry said.

He took a forkful and chewed for quite a while. "I like the flavor. The mushrooms don't overwhelm the taste of the cheese."

He took another small chunk. He made a face as he swallowed. "But I'm not happy with the texture," he said. He turned to the other two judges. "Are you finding it dry?"

They both nodded.

"It's overcooked," Jake said. "That's the problem."

"Thank you, Debra and Miller," Hess said, taking the plates from the judges. "You may go back to your kitchen."

Hess handed the plates to Morgan, the assistant. Then he crossed the room and picked up the dish by Ashli and Nathan. He placed it on the judges' table, and they helped themselves to slices.

"This is Ashli and Nathan," Hess said. He turned to them. "Tell the judges about your creation."

"We made a bacon omelet. And then we made a separate dish from the mushrooms and cheese."

"We call it a mushroom melt," Nathan added. "We think it makes a good side dish for the omelet."

The judges all chewed in silence for a while.

I turned to Nicole. "Show-offs," I whispered. "That mushroom thing probably tastes like paste."

"The omelet is perfection," Mary declared, closing her eyes and smiling. The other two judges nodded.

"Fluffy and very flavorful," Jake said.

"Just the right amount of bacon," Larry added.

My heart leaped into my mouth. *Ashli and Nathan can't win this!* I thought. *It just wouldn't be fair.*

Nicole squeezed my wrist. She must have seen how upset I was. "I'm sure our omelet is better," she whispered. "You and I are pros, remember?"

"This is very good work," Larry said to Ashli and Nathan. "Very impressive."

All three judges applauded. Ashli and Nathan took little bows. They had mile-wide grins on their faces.

Hess picked up our omelet plate in both hands to carry it to the judges' table. But as he started to walk, Nathan shot a hand out and bumped him in the side.

"Whoa!" Hess let out a cry. He fumbled for the plate and caught it without spilling anything.

"Oops. Sorry," Nathan said quickly to Hess. "I didn't see you there."

A burst of anger shot through my body. Both of my hands clenched into tight fists. Nicole had her teeth gritted and was scowling hard at Nathan.

He paid no attention to her. He and Ashli exchanged grins.

The omelet looked a little lopsided when Hess set it down in front of the judges. They divided it up onto their plates. "What do you call this?" Larry asked.

"It's a cheese omelet," I answered. "With mushrooms and bacon. Simple."

"Simple, but I'm sure, delicious," Mary said, flashing her nice smile.

All three lifted their forks and began to chew. I watched with my fists still clenched as they took their second bite.

Mary was the first to grab her neck.

She made a choking sound, squeezed her throat, and jumped to her feet.

I saw Jake's eyes bulge. He groaned and coughed. Then he leaped to his feet, gasping and choking.

Larry shut his eyes tight and screamed. "Burning!" he choked out. "My throat . . . burning!" He tried to stand up. But lost his balance.

And collapsed to the floor on his side. His chair fell on top of him.

Mary and Jake were bent over, gagging and choking. Their faces were tomato red and tears ran down their cheeks.

"Hellllp," Mary groaned. "Helllllp me!"

Larry struggled to sit up. Holding his throat with one hand, he began to scream. "My throat is burning! Somebody—HELP! Burning! Too hot! . . ."

Watching them, I felt sick. I grabbed the top of the counter to keep from sinking to the floor.

Nicole's mouth gaped open. Her eyes were wide with shock, and I could see she was trembling.

I turned to her. "Nicole," I cried. "What have we done?"

11

Later. Much later. It seemed like *years* later.

Nicole and I were in my bedroom. I sat tensely on the edge of my desk chair. She was sprawled on the carpet with her back against the bed.

I felt shaky and strange, like I could burst into tears at any moment.

Nicole's black hair fell in tangles around her face. Her cheeks were very pale. She kept clasping and unclasping her hands.

"Well, *that* went well!" I said. I was trying to keep it light. But it didn't come out very funny.

Nicole started to say something. But Toby burst into the room, screaming like a wild man.

I covered both ears. "Stop it. Why did you scream like that?" I cried.

His eyes flashed. "Did I scare you? I was trying to scare you."

"No. You just annoyed us," I said. "Go away, Toby. We're not in the mood—"

He stepped right over Nicole and grabbed my backpack off the bed.

"Put that down!" I screamed.

"Where is it?" he said. "My birthday present. It's in here, isn't it?"

I suddenly remembered the cans of Monster Blood. I'd forgotten all about them.

"No present," I said. "I didn't get you a present this year."

"Liar!" He tore open the flap and began pawing through the backpack.

"Give that to me!" I shouted. I scrambled to my feet and dove for it.

"Hey—!" Toby let out a shout as I swiped the backpack from his hands. He made a two-handed grab for it, but I tossed it to Nicole.

Toby swung around and started toward Nicole—when my mother's voice from the hallway interrupted. "Toby, come here. Right now. I need to talk to you about your party."

Nicole tossed the backpack to me, and I hugged it tightly in my arms. "Get lost, pest."

Toby stuck his tongue out at me and made a long spitting noise. Then he stomped out of the room. I closed the door behind him.

"I've got to hide the Monster Blood," I said. I glanced around the room.

"Your closet is the best bet," Nicole said. "Does he go in your closet?"

"He goes everywhere," I said. "He's a total snoop. It's unbelievable."

I pulled out the two cans of Monster Blood and carried them to the back of my closet. I have a very long, narrow clothes closet with a small dresser at the back wall.

I shoved the two cans as far as they could go under the dresser. Then I took a few pairs of dirty jeans I had piled on the closet floor and stuffed them under there to completely hide the Monster Blood.

I sat down again across from Nicole, and we stared at each other for a long time. "I'm just speechless," I said finally.

Nicole sighed. "Sascha, what can we say? We're out. We're toast. We're losers." She sighed again. "And it's all because of Nathan and Ashli."

"Wish we could prove it," I said. "Wish we could prove they did it."

"What if we could?" Nicole said. "Then what? We go and report them to the TV people? Who is going to believe us? It's Nathan and Ashli's word against ours."

I realized I was pounding my sides with my fists. I took a long, slow breath and uncurled my hands. "At least no one *died*!" I said. "That judge Larry was choking so hard, I thought he was a goner."

Nicole shook her head. She pushed back her hair. "They were all better by the time the paramedics arrived," she said. "I mean, their throats were all burned . . ."

"But at least they stopped gagging and coughing," I said. "They were breathing almost normally."

Nicole gripped her stomach. "I'm suddenly starving. Do you have any snacks or anything?"

"There's some tortilla chips and salsa in the kitchen," I said.

She rolled her eyes. "As long as it's not too spicy!"

"Haha," I muttered. I led the way downstairs.

I couldn't stop thinking about what happened at the TV studio. Nicole and I both knew that Nathan had poured a whole bottle of yellow hot sauce into our omelet.

The poor, choking judges were in terrible pain. Even after the paramedics had treated them, two judges—Mary and Larry—couldn't speak at all. And Jake could only whisper.

Hess was frantic. He kept running back and forth, shouting at his assistants, making phone calls. Then he told us to gather up our backpacks. He led us to the studio doors.

"Of course, you're off the show," he said, keeping his eyes down, not looking at us. "I will assume what you did was an accident. But I have to warn you . . ." He leaned closer and whispered, "If the judges have medical expenses, your parents will have to pay them."

45

"But—but—" I sputtered.

He swung the glass door open and practically pushed us out. "You two should probably take up another hobby," he said. "Maybe hang gliding?"

Did he think that was funny?

He closed the door behind us.

We walked home with our heads down, not saying a word.

Now, back in my kitchen, the salsa and tortilla chips were tasty, but they couldn't distract us from the horrible thing Nathan and Ashli had done to us.

"They are such total cheaters," I said. "And they're going to get away with it."

I opened the fridge door and pulled out a can of Coke. I started to hand it to Nicole. But a shrill scream from upstairs made me drop the can.

"HELP ME! HELLLLLP ME!"

Toby!

12

"Toby! What's wrong?" I shouted.

I turned to run to the stairs and stumbled over the Coke can. Nicole caught me before I fell. We both took off running.

"Help me! Hurry! HELLLP!"

Toby's frightened screams rang in my ears as I took the stairs two at a time. I burst into his room, breathing hard. Nicole ran in right behind me.

"What is it? What's wrong?" I cried, gasping for breath.

Toby stood in the middle of his room, waving his right arm up and down. It took me a few seconds to see the bright green blob around his wrist. He shoved it in front of my face. "Look at it! I can't pull it off."

Nicole bent down and lifted an open blue can off the rug. She squinted at the label. "It's the Monster Blood."

Toby tugged hard at the shiny green gunk.

"I—I found my birthday gift," he stammered. "You're such a terrible hider, Sascha. It's awesome. But it climbed up from my hand and won't let go."

"Serves you right for sneaking into my closet and taking it," I said.

Nicole laughed. "Toby, you really think we'll fall for *anything*, don't you!"

"No. You have to help me. I'm not joking. It really is moving up my arm, Sascha. And it's holding on tight."

I stared at it. The green blob was an inch or two above his wrist now. Had it really moved?

"Toby, you pushed it up. You can't fool us," I said.

He grabbed it with his left hand and tugged with all his strength. "Don't you *see*?" he demanded in a high, shrill voice. "It's totally stuck to me. It won't come off!"

Nicole laughed again. "You're such a good actor. It's just green slime. That's all it is."

"YOU try to pull it off!" Toby screamed. "Come on! YOU try!"

He stuck his arm out. I grabbed one side of the green ring and Nicole grabbed the other. The Monster Blood felt warm in my hand.

We both pulled.

It stretched a little but it didn't break off. I tried using both hands. "Pull!" I shouted at Toby. "Pull back!"

I tugged one way. He pulled the other.

"Hey—!" I tried to slide my hand away. But the sticky, warm Monster Blood stretched with it. "Hey—let go!"

"My hand is stuck, too!" Nicole cried. "Oh . . . weird. *Weird.*"

The sticky green goo spread over the back of my hand, tugging it deeper inside it. "It's *swallowing* my hand!" I cried. "Look! It's spreading out. Like it's ALIVE!"

13

Toby laughed. "It's awesome!"

I glared at him. "A minute ago, you were screaming for help."

"But this is the coolest slime ever!" he cried.

I swung my arm hard—and my hand came free with a loud *pop*.

The green goo had climbed over my brother's arm up to his elbow. "I can feel it. I think it's breathing!" he said.

Nicole slid her hand free and wiped it on the side of her shorts. "It's . . . yuck," she choked out. "It's too scary . . ."

"Let's just get it back in the can," I said.

"It's so warm," Toby said. "Like I'm wearing a sweater." His smile faded. "Hey—I can feel it tightening around my arm. Get it off! Hurry!"

"Make up your mind," I said. "Do you think it's awesome or frightening?"

"Both," he murmured. "Hurry. Get it off me."

"I . . . I don't want to touch it again," Nicole said.

I had an idea. I crossed the hall to my room and pulled two pairs of latex gloves from a bottom drawer in my dresser.

I'd used them for a school science project. I don't know why I kept them. Maybe they would come in handy now.

I rushed back to Toby's room. The Monster Blood had stretched up to his shoulder. Nicole was staring at it in horror, her hands pressed against the sides of her face.

I handed her a pair of gloves. "Put these on. Maybe the gloves won't stick to it."

Toby grabbed a hunk of the green gunk with his free hand and tugged. It stretched like bubblegum and wrapped around his hand.

Nicole and I went to work with our gloved hands. We rolled the goo down from Toby's shoulder. The gloves didn't stick. I pulled a big chunk free. Then another.

"Sascha, you're a genius," Nicole said. "These gloves are working. We're getting it off Toby's skin."

"Don't wreck it," Toby said. "I want to show it to the kids at my birthday party."

"No way," I said. "Are you *kidding* me? This is going right back to the store. You can't keep it."

"But it's my birthday gift!" he wailed.

I slid another chunk of Monster Blood from his arm. "I'll get you a better gift," I told him. "Something that doesn't try to swallow you alive."

51

"Toby, you're weird," Nicole said. "You can't hate it and like it at the same time."

He stared at her. "Seriously?"

Nicole and I now held big blobs of Monster Blood in our hands. "Go wash your arm," I told my brother. "We got almost all of it off."

He hurried to the bathroom.

I spotted the can on the floor beside his bed. "Come on. Let's shove this stuff back in the can."

Nicole and I dropped to our knees. I lowered my hand to the open can and started to push the green gunk inside it.

"Sascha, it's not going to fit," she said.

"Huh?"

She was right. I had filled up the can. But I still had a big handful of the stuff. And Nicole had two handfuls.

"It . . . grew," I said.

"And look at it," Nicole said in a trembling voice. "It's still growing. I can see it."

I could feel the panic rise to my throat. I suddenly had to force myself to breathe. "Wh-what are we going to do?" I stammered.

14

And then I heard voices. And footsteps coming up the stairs.

Mom and Dad.

"Don't tell them about this!" I cried.

Nicole's mouth dropped open. "But—"

"Quick. Hide it," I said. "They always say I buy terrible gifts."

She squinted at me. "But—"

"They're going to blame me," I said. "If this is a disaster, they will ground me for a month. Hide it!"

I heard them coming closer. I spun around and shoved the Monster Blood and my gloves under Toby's bed. "Quick—" I pushed Nicole toward the bed, and she slid her handful of green gunk and gloves under the bed, too.

We both turned as Mom and Dad stepped into the room.

"Hey," I said. "What's up?" I forced a smile. Could they see how frantic I was?

"What are you two doing? Where's Toby?" Dad said, glancing around the room.

"Washing his hands," I said.

Mom's mouth dropped open. "Washing his hands in the middle of the day? Without being forced to? Is he sick?"

"No. He's not sick," I said. "His hands were dirty."

"Well, why are you in his room?" Dad asked. He kept looking around. I glanced under the bed to check if the Monster Blood could be seen.

"We were talking about Toby's birthday gift," Nicole chimed in.

That was true.

"Don't ask him what he wants," Dad said. "He has a list of at least a hundred PlayStation games." Dad chuckled. "I told him we were buying him pajamas."

"He didn't think that was funny," Mom added.

"Nicole, did you want to stay for dinner?" Dad asked. "We want to hear all about the cooking show tryout."

"No, you don't!" I exclaimed. "Believe me. You don't."

"Thanks. But I'd better get home," Nicole said. I knew she didn't want to be around when I explained the disaster at the TV studio to my parents.

Mom shook her head. "I can't believe we invited

ten of Toby's friends for his birthday party Saturday morning. The house will never be the same. We'll have to *move!*"

I laughed. That was a pretty good joke for Mom. Or was she joking?

"Sascha, will you be able to help out with Toby's party?" Dad asked.

Would I like to cut off my nose and duct-tape it to the back of my head?

"Uh . . . I'm not sure," I said. Which meant definitely *no*.

Mom and Dad finally went back downstairs.

Nicole and I dropped down to the floor and peered at the big puddle of Monster Blood under the bed. I gasped. "It's still growing. What are we going to do with this?"

"We'll have to take it back to the store tomorrow," Nicole said. "There's something wrong with it. That freak Bardo *has* to take it back."

We pulled our gloves back on. Then we ducked under the bed and began to scoop up the Monster Blood. It stuck to the carpet, and we had to work like crazy to scrape it out.

"Now what do we do with it?" Nicole demanded. "It's way too big for the can it came in."

We both stared at the shiny green goo for a long moment. "Wait right here," I said. I climbed to my feet and ran across the hall to my room.

I lifted my backpack off the bed and carried it

into Toby's room. "We'll just stuff it in here," I said. I pulled open the flap. "Then it will be easy to carry to the toy store after school tomorrow."

"Just remember not to put your books in there," Nicole warned.

I snickered. "Good advice."

It was a struggle. But we managed to push every drop of the sticky gunk into the backpack. I closed the flap and carefully snapped the latch. Then I hung it on my closet door.

"Sascha—dinnertime!" Mom's shout burst up from the kitchen downstairs.

Nicole sighed and wiped sweat off her forehead. "Well, this was an adventure," she said, rolling her eyes.

"I've had enough adventure for one day," I said.

I walked Nicole downstairs. "Can you come to the toy store with me after school tomorrow?" I asked. "I really don't want to be in that creepy place alone."

"No prob," she said, and headed out the door.

Dinner wasn't any fun. I had to tell my parents why Nicole and I were kicked out of the tryout.

"But you should have told the producers what Nathan and Ashli did to you," Dad said. "You should have—"

"Don't listen to him," Mom interrupted. "You did the right thing. Those two kids would just deny it. And you had no proof."

"Nathan's father cheats at poker," Dad said. "I

caught him dealing from under the deck twice."

Mom frowned at him. "Let's change the subject," she said. Mom doesn't like unpleasantness of any kind.

"Yeah. Let's talk about my birthday," Toby said. His face was covered in spaghetti sauce. He eats like a dog, with his face in the plate. "How many games are you getting me?"

I tuned out and somehow made it through dinner.

I did a little homework. Then I went to bed early. What a stressful day. It made my bones feel tired! So many things went wrong. First the disaster at the TV show. Then the Monster Blood mess with Toby . . .

I just wanted to drift off to sleep and escape for a while.

But just as I was fading away, a sound across my room brought me back. I sat up, instantly alert.

I held my breath and listened.

Gurgle . . . gurrrrgle . . . squish . . .

Wet sucking sounds. Like in a swamp or something.

Like a gurgling stomach when you're hungry.

Gurrrgle . . . gurgle . . . squish . . . squish . . .

I wrapped the pillow around my head, but I couldn't block out the horrifying sounds . . .

Gurrrgle . . . gurgle . . . squish . . . squish . . .

15

The next day at school, Nicole and I ran into Nathan in the hall outside the lunchroom. We quickly turned to go the other way. But he had already seen us.

A sick grin crossed his face. "Hey," he said. "Are you going in to lunch? I hear you girls like spicy food." He laughed. He thinks he's a riot.

"Haha," I said sarcastically. "You're not funny, Nathan. You're sick."

"Cheaters don't win," Nicole said through gritted teeth.

"Of course they do!" Nathan shot back. "But . . . I don't know any cheaters."

"I'm looking at one," Nicole replied. "We know what you did."

"You owe us big-time, Nathan," I said. "For not snitching on you and Ashli."

Nathan shrugged. "Should I know what you're talking about? Because I don't."

I raised both fists. I wanted to pound him. I wanted to smash the sick grin off his face.

"You know what would be cool?" Nathan said. "After we win the TV contest... Ashli and I could come over and give you both cooking lessons." His grin spread across his face.

Somehow, I kept myself from hitting him. I guess it's because I'm a nonviolent person.

I let out an angry groan. Then I pushed Nathan out of the way, and Nicole and I strode into the lunchroom. We were both steaming. "What a jerk. My stomach is one big knot," Nicole said. "How am I supposed to eat?"

"We'll find a way to pay those two cheaters back," I said. "I know we will."

But I didn't have any ideas. Even though I thought about it the rest of the afternoon.

I was still daydreaming about revenge when the final bell rang. I gathered up my stuff and turned to Nicole. "Are you coming with me to the toy store?"

She nodded. "Yes. Let's DO this!"

We hurried out of the classroom, turned down the front hall, and headed toward my locker.

I was nearly there when I stopped short. A gasp escaped my throat. And then I opened my mouth in a scream of horror.

16

I gripped Nicole's arm and gaped at the wide green puddle on the floor in front of my locker. "Oh nooooo." I knew at once what it was.

The Monster Blood.

I'd left the backpack in my locker, and now the green goo was oozing down the front of the locker from the vents in the door. And spreading out in a thick puddle on the hall floor. I should have known the backpack wouldn't hold it.

I heard startled cries all around . . .

"Eeeuuw! Somebody was sick!"

"Ohh, it reeks."

"Do you believe it? Someone puked all over that locker."

Ashli stopped to gawk at the mess. She grinned at us. "Looks like someone else tried to sample your food!" She hurried away, laughing at her own dumb joke.

Kids stepped out of the way as they passed.

They were eager to leave school, so they hurried away from the mess.

Ploppppp.

I gasped as a big blob of it pushed out of the locker and smacked the floor.

My whole body shuddered. "It's—it's totally out of control. What are we going to do?"

"I think I have something we can put it in," Nicole said. "I'll be right back." She took off running down the hall.

I crossed my arms in front of me to keep from shaking. More kids hurried past. Nathan came walking up. He squinted at the green puddle. "Whoa! Sascha? Are you sick? What did you eat for lunch?"

"I didn't do that!" I snapped.

He shrugged and strutted away.

Nicole returned carrying a big black canvas tote bag. "It was in the science lab," she explained. "I carried my project to school in it."

"It's big enough," I said.

"And look." Nicole held up two metal scoops. "I found these in there, too."

"Great. Let's hurry," I said. "We don't know when the toy store closes."

We dropped to our knees and began scooping the Monster Blood off the floor and emptying it into the big tote bag. It wasn't easy to scoop. The gunk clung to the floor, and it stuck to the scoops.

It made sick plopping and squishing sounds as we dumped it into the bag. I opened the locker door, and a tall wave of Monster Blood came pouring out.

"This is . . . impossible," I said, sighing. "That toy store guy better give us our money back."

Somehow Nicole had Monster Blood tangled in a thick strand of her black hair. She struggled to pull it out with both hands.

"This stuff is dangerous," I said. I turned to help her. I held the strand of hair and plucked at the green goo. "That guy Bardo is putting the public in danger."

"Let's just get the Monster Blood back to him," Nicole said, sweeping her hair behind her head.

I can't say how long we worked. It seemed like *years*. The hall was empty by the time we had all the Monster Blood stuffed into the tote bag.

The bag didn't have a zipper, so we couldn't completely close it. We fastened the snaps on the flap as best we could. I slammed the locker door shut, and we made our way to the exit.

It was a gray day, dark clouds hanging low overhead. The air felt steamy wet, as if rain was on the way.

I tried to carry the bulging bag in one hand, but it was too heavy. So I pulled the straps over my shoulder and walked with it under my arm.

We crossed the street and started up the next

block. A soccer ball came bouncing in front of us, and I nearly tripped over it. I grabbed the bag tightly against my side to keep any gunk from spilling out. Some boys from the elementary school came running after the ball.

"Want me to carry it for a while?" Nicole was still pulling at her hair.

"I'm okay," I said. "It's a short walk." I remembered the toy store was about two blocks from the TV studio where we had our kitchen disaster.

On the lawn across from us, two squirrels were battling over an acorn. Nicole and I were less than three feet away, and they didn't seem to care. One squirrel stuffed the nut into its mouth and stood daring the other to do something about it.

"Squirrels are rodents," I said. "But everyone thinks they're adorable."

Nicole didn't reply. She stared ahead to the next block, searching for the toy store. The bag began to feel heavier and heavier. I was glad we were approaching the store.

Only it wasn't at the next corner.

"I could swear this was the block," Nicole said, scratching her head.

I set the bag down on the sidewalk to rest my aching shoulder. I peered across the street. The store on the corner was a dry cleaner. The store next to it was vacant.

"I guess it's one more block," I said. I felt a cold

raindrop on my forehead. I hoisted up the tote bag. "Hurry. We don't want to get drenched."

The wind picked up, and I felt more raindrops on my head. We leaned into the whistling gusts and made our way down the block. We passed two houses that were dark and a small park with fresh tulips swaying from side to side in the wind.

"There it is, I think!" Nicole said, pointing.

But she was wrong. The corner store had a sign in front of its window: SHOE REPAIR WHILE-YOU-WAIT.

A small diner stood next to it, with a blinking neon sign over the door that said EATS & TREATS.

I set the bag down again. "I don't remember those stores," I said. I had a sudden heavy feeling in the pit of my stomach. "I've lived in this neighborhood forever and . . ." My voice trailed off.

"I've gone by here a hundred times," Nicole said, squinting at the two stores. "I don't remember seeing these stores at all."

The rain began to patter the sidewalk. I pulled my jacket tighter. I wished I'd worn a hoodie or something to cover my head.

"Did we go the wrong way?" Nicole asked. She swung around and peered in the other direction. "No way. This is the right corner. But where's that stupid toy store?" Her voice trembled.

I felt kind of shaky, too.

I gazed up at the dark sky. "We're going to get soaked," I said. "Maybe we should just go home and try tomorrow."

Nicole opened her mouth to reply. But a loud shout made her stop.

We turned to see a man running full speed on the sidewalk, waving both hands and shouting at us. "Stop right there! Don't MOVE!"

17

The man's dark sports jacket whipped behind him in the wind. He crossed the street without looking for traffic, waving his arms frantically.

Heston Hill. Hess. From the TV show.

It took a short while to recognize him with his hair blowing wildly about his face. He stopped in front of us, gasping for breath. He bent forward and pressed his hands on his knees.

"You—you scared me," I stammered.

"Me too," Nicole said.

"Sorry." He still hadn't caught his breath. Finally, he stood up. He flattened his short hair down with one hand. "I was just so surprised to see you two."

He brushed raindrops off his eyebrows. His gaze went from Nicole to me. "What are you doing here?"

"We had an errand to run," I said, glancing at the tote bag beside me on the sidewalk.

"Well, this could be a stroke of luck," he said. "You see, I have a problem. Maybe you two can help me with it."

"Problem?" I said.

He let out a long whoosh of air. Despite the cool air, he was sweating. I could see he was in some kind of panic.

"Well . . . uh . . . You see," he said. "We just started taping the show, and one of our cooking teams got sick."

"Was it Nathan and Ashli?" I asked eagerly. I crossed my fingers.

"Not them," Hess answered. "A new team. We had to send them home. And we have to do the first show today."

He leaned forward and spoke in a soft voice, just above a whisper. As if he was telling us a secret. "Can you two step in and take their place?"

"Huh?" I gasped.

Nicole scrunched up her face. "Excuse me?"

Hess raised both hands, as if surrendering. "All is forgiven," he said. "Seriously. What happened, happened. I'm sure it was an accident. We'll just forget about it."

I swallowed. I couldn't believe what he was saying. "You want us to go be on the show *now*?" I said in a shrill voice.

"We can go back?" Nicole echoed my question.

Hess nodded. "Yes. Now. A fresh start. Only this is for real. Not a tryout. This is the real show."

He pressed his hands together as if he was praying. "Will you do it?"

Guess what our answer was?

SLAPPY HERE, EVERYONE.

Well, well. The girls are going to get a second chance.

A second chance to mess up! Hahahaha.

How are they going to win? They wouldn't dare *cheat* against Ashli and Nathan—would they?

They wouldn't dare use Monster Blood to win that big-money prize.

That would be disgusting—wouldn't it?

Do we want this story to turn disgusting?

Of course not! Hahahaha.

18

I heard one of the judges groan as Nicole and I walked into the TV studio. I think it was Jake. None of them had smiles on their faces as we walked past their table.

In their kitchen space, Ashli and Nathan both made faces and flashed us thumbs-downs as we stepped once again into the kitchen next to them.

I set the bulging tote bag under the kitchen counter. Nicole and I took off our wet jackets and tossed them under the counter, too.

Two new kids were in the third kitchen. Hess introduced them to us: Jackson and Sunday. They weren't from our school. But they seemed to be about our age.

Sunday was about a foot taller than Jackson. They both wore matching navy-blue polo shirts that said *Go, Master Chefs* in big white letters on the front.

Nicole and I both tried to fix our hair with our hands. There was no mirror, so we didn't know how we looked. It was our first time on TV. Exciting. But Hess was so eager to start shooting, he didn't give us a chance to make ourselves ready.

"Places, everyone," the voice on the loudspeaker boomed. "Emergency time is over. We have a show to do."

Hess stood next to one of the camera operators, clipboard in his hand. Morgan, his assistant, stepped in front of the camera carrying a clapboard. You know. One of those things they clap together and say something like "Take six."

Beside us, Ashli leaned over her counter. She pointed to Nicole and me. "Hess," she shouted, "shouldn't you search their backpacks to make sure they didn't bring hot sauce?"

That made the camera guys laugh. The judges didn't crack a smile.

"We don't need hot sauce to beat you two," I snapped.

But Nicole still looked really annoyed. She leaned close and whispered, "Are they just going to make fun of us for the whole show?"

"Stay cool," I whispered, too. "I have a plan. I know exactly how we're going to pay Ashli and Nathan back."

71

19

A few seconds later, everyone in the studio went quiet, and the show began. Hess stepped in front of the cameras with a big grin on his face.

"Welcome, everyone, to *Kids' Big Chef Food Fights*. We have three teams of chefs, and they are ready to do battle. Let's see who can COOK— and who will get the HOOK. At the end of the show, two of these teams will go home. And one team will go home with the Silver Spatula, a prize worth two thousand dollars!"

Hess motioned around the three kitchen areas. "Now let's meet our teams. We'll start with you." He pointed to Ashli and Nathan.

"I'm Nathan and she's Ashli," Nathan said. "We are from Adam Driver Middle School, and we are the winners of this contest!"

Hess's grin grew wider. "I like your confidence, Nathan!" he exclaimed.

Jackson and Sunday went next. They were from

a private school across town from ours. Sunday waved a spatula in the air and said, "We want to turn this into silver!"

Hess replied, "I like that. The battle has begun, everyone!"

One of the cameras moved toward Nicole and me. "I'm Sascha and she's Nicole," I announced. "We don't have anything clever to say. That's because we came to *cook*, not talk!"

Hess nodded and smiled. He seemed to like that.

My heart was fluttering, and my hands were cold and wet. Nicole must have seen how nervous I was. She put a hand on mine and said, "Sascha, you'll feel better as soon as we start cooking."

"Here are our kitchen battle rules," Hess said. He was reading off a teleprompter. "Each team must cook three dishes—lunch, dinner, and dessert. Three rounds. The winning team in each round is awarded ten points—plus an extra ten for dessert! Highest number of points wins the contest!"

Courtney, the other assistant, brought a box to each table.

"Okay, teams, open your ingredients boxes for lunch—and let the kitchen war begin!"

Nicole and I opened the lid together and peered in at the ingredients. Macaroni noodles, cheese, tomatoes, green peppers, and ground beef.

I drummed my fingers on the countertop. "What

do you think, Nicole? It has to be a lunch dish."

We studied the ingredients a while longer.

"How about a pasta casserole?" I said.

"Yes. A baked casserole. Maybe put the ground beef on the bottom?"

"Excellent," I said, starting to feel better. "We can do this."

The video cameras were moving in and out, sliding from one team to another. I reached into the box to start removing the ingredients—but Nathan leaned over our counter.

"Try not to choke the judges this time," he said. Then he tossed his hands up and went, "WHOOOPS!"

He pretended to fall—and knocked our ingredients box to the floor.

"Hey, you jerk—!" I shouted.

The cameras swung around to capture the fuss.

I motioned to Hess. I thought he might stop everything. Instead, the big grin returned to his face. "The battle has begun!" he exclaimed into the cameras. "As Shakespeare once said, 'All's fair in love and cooking!'"

That didn't make any sense to me, but I didn't have time to think about it. Nicole and I scrambled to pick up the ingredients and line them up on our counter.

"Did Hess see what Nathan did?" Nicole asked.

"Hess doesn't care," I told her. "He likes it when things get crazy." I brought my face close to hers and whispered, "Just be cool. Nathan's time will come. I promise."

I turned the oven on to BAKE at 350 degrees. Then we set to work, preparing the ingredients for our casserole dish. We worked well together. It didn't take long to get everything sliced and diced and spooned into the casserole dish. I put the lid on and slid it into the oven.

"Ten minutes left, chefs!" Hess announced. "Ten minutes, everyone!"

I turned to Nicole. "Our dish should be cooked by then," I said. "We lost some time because Nathan knocked our stuff to the floor."

"Ten minutes should be perfect," she answered.

I gazed about the room. Sunday and Jackson were stirring a big pot on their stove with wooden spoons. On our other side, Ashli and Nathan were having an argument.

I couldn't catch the words. Their backs were turned. But Ashli was angrily waving a metal whisk at Nathan. He backed up to the counter with both hands in the air.

The cameras moved around, recording the last-minute activity. Hess stood in a corner of the studio, talking with Courtney and Morgan. He had his eyes on the big round clock on the wall.

"OKAY! TIME IS UP!" he shouted. "All teams, stop work. The judges are ready. Prepare to present your dishes."

I could feel my heart start to beat faster. I took

a deep breath, fighting back my nervousness.

I pulled on oven gloves and lifted the casserole dish from the oven. I carried it to the counter.

I turned to Nicole. She had her fingers crossed on both hands. "Here goes," I said. "Hope we do better than last time."

20

I watched the three judges—Larry, Mary, and Jake—pull their chairs closer to their table. They smoothed down their hair, and adjusted their outfits, and cleared their throats. Getting ready to go on camera.

I told myself not to get nervous. Our casserole dish was solid and simple. But did *you* ever tell yourself not to get nervous? Then you know it doesn't work at all. In fact, it makes you even more stressed out!

Hess announced that Sunday and Jackson were to be judged first. Morgan took the tall metal pot off their counter and carried it to the judges' table.

Courtney set down spoons and soup bowls. Then she ladled the steaming liquid from the pot into the three bowls.

"Sunday and Jackson, please tell the judges what you have made," Hess said.

They gazed at each other. They couldn't decide which of them should talk. Then they both started to talk at once. That made them both laugh.

"Sunday, why don't *you* explain the dish?" Hess suggested.

She swallowed. "Well, we made a soup. It's a tomato pasta soup with meat."

"Kind of a chili," Jackson added. "It's chili and soup. We invented it."

That made Nathan laugh out loud. He's so totally rude. "Did they invent chili or soup?" he whispered to Ashli. And she laughed, too.

I realized I was gripping the counter edge tightly with both hands. I lowered my hands and backed away.

The judges took their time tasting the chili-soup. Larry had a smile on his face as he tried three or four spoonfuls. Mary had her face scrunched up and seemed to be thinking hard. Jake tasted the dish, then poked his spoon around the food in the bowl, examining it.

Hess stepped in front of a camera. "Okay, judges—what do you think?" he said. "Larry, let's start with you."

Larry set down his spoon. "Well, I like the *idea* of the soup," he said. "And I think it tastes pretty good. But to me, the tomato overwhelms everything else. I can't taste the peppers or the cheese. I think you should call this tomato soup.

You haven't succeeded with your chili idea."

"I agree with Larry," Mary said. "And I'm finding the soup rather thin. I think you need to spice it up. The green peppers aren't enough to give it flavor."

"I loved it," Jake chimed in. "Of course, I love tomato soup. It's my favorite. And I think the beef and the pasta and peppers are just an added treat."

He turned to the other judges. "I would like it a little hotter," he said. "I like a soup that burns your tongue—don't you?"

The other two judges shook their heads no.

Hess stepped up again. "Thank you, judges. And thank you, Chef Sunday and Chef Jackson. Next up, let's sample the dish by Ashli and Nathan. What dish have you prepared?"

"It's an eggless frittata," Nathan said. "It's an Italian dish, a little like an omelet."

"Only, an omelet is cooked fast," Ashli added. "A frittata is cooked slower. And a frittata doesn't have to be served right away. It can be saved for later."

"A frittata is different from a quiche," Nathan added. "A quiche has a crust, while a frittata is crustless."

"Nathan and I have been working for a long time on an eggless frittata," Ashli added. "And I think we've perfected it."

They both grinned, very pleased with their little lecture.

"Well, I see you two have done your homework," Hess said. "Now let's see if your frittata is as good as your knowledge of Italian cooking."

Each judge placed a slice of the frittata on their plate and began to sample it. "Mmmmm," Jake hummed, chewing a mouthful. He kept nodding his head. I guessed he liked it.

"Nice texture," Mary muttered to the other two. They all chewed some more. Jake lowered his head and sniffed it for a while.

"Well, judges?" Hess said. "What's your verdict?"

"Two thumbs up," Larry said. "I can't find anything to criticize. I would like this if it was served to me in a restaurant."

"Wow. That's high praise," Hess said.

Nathan and Ashli slapped a high five.

"I'm especially impressed with the texture," Mary said. "It's light and moist, and the taste of the ingredients seems in perfect balance. I don't miss the eggs at all."

"I think it's a little too crumbly," Jake said, poking the frittata on his plate with his fork. "But you had so little time to bake it, I'm very impressed with it." He also flashed two thumbs-ups.

Nicole bumped my arm. "They're going to win," she whispered.

"No way," I whispered back. "I think we've got this one."

That was a lie. But I didn't want Nicole to give up before we were even judged. Mainly because if Nicole gave up, I'd give up, too.

I suddenly realized Hess had turned to us. "What have you made for us, Chefs Nicole and Sascha?" he asked.

Nicole bumped me again. I guessed she wanted me to do the talking.

"It's a pasta casserole," I said. "Very simple. I guess you'd call it comfort food. Perfect for a cold winter day."

"And it's a meal in one," Nicole added.

The judges all dipped into the casserole dish and placed a portion onto their plates. Jake lowered his head and sniffed it. "Mmmmmmm. Interesting," he said.

I realized I was holding my breath. Every muscle in my body had tightened, and my teeth were clamped tightly together.

Yeah, I guess you could say I was nervous.

Beside me, Nicole gripped the counter and didn't blink or move or say a word. We both watched the judges raise their forks to their mouths and start to sample the casserole.

They're going to love it, I told myself. *They're going to love it.*

Mary was the first to react. Her eyes went

wide and she opened her mouth and uttered, "Oh. Ugggh."

Jake coughed and started to sputter.

And Larry moved a big chunk in his mouth— and *spit it out* with a loud SPLAAAT onto the table.

21

I gasped and grabbed Nicole's hand. I could feel the blood come rushing up to my head. I thought I might faint.

"It's . . . *cold*!" Jake exclaimed.

"Cold and hard," Mary said, spitting a mouthful into her napkin.

I forced myself to breathe. Beside me, Nicole had gone pale. Her chin was quivering, as if she was about to cry.

Jake climbed to his feet, wiping his mouth with his napkin. He turned to us. "Sascha and Nicole, you forgot one little thing," he said. "You forgot to cook it."

"But—but—" I sputtered.

"Th-that's impossible!" Nicole cried.

I turned and darted to the oven. I opened the door and reached my hand inside.

Cold.

I gazed at the dials on the front of the stove. OFF. The oven was off, but we hadn't turned it off.

Whoa, wait. I remembered setting it to 350 degrees. That was the first thing I did before Nicole and I started to work with the ingredients.

Hold on a sec. I had a sudden flash. Ashli and Nathan.

I spun around. They both had their backs turned to Nicole and me.

Why were they facing the wrong way? So we wouldn't see their laughter?

I turned back to Nicole. "It had to be our friends over there again," I said, motioning to Ashli and Nathan. "When we were preparing the ingredients, one of them must have clicked off our oven."

"Grrrrr." Nicole growled like an angry tiger. Her eyes lit up with anger. She started toward them. But I held her back.

"Wait," I said. "Just . . . wait."

I turned to Hess. "Are we going to do that round over again? I mean, since . . ."

He shook his head. "No. No time. We're going to start rolling again. I'm going to announce our first-round winners—Ashli and Nathan. Then we're going to reset for the dinner round."

He must have seen how upset we were, because he walked over to our kitchen. "Don't give up, girls," he said softly. "You aren't out of it. You still have two rounds to go."

Nicole pointed to Ashli and Nathan. "Listen, Hess. Those two—"

He interrupted her. "Yes, they're good chefs. But you can do better. Just keep telling yourselves that." He walked away before Nicole could say anything more.

Nicole let out another tiger growl.

I turned to Ashli and Nathan. They still had their backs turned to us. I saw Nathan's shoulders roll up and down. Yes. He was laughing.

Nicole grabbed my arm. "Sascha—what are we going to do?"

22

Everyone moved back into place and the cameras began to glide in and out again. "Second round!" Hess announced. "The dinner round."

Courtney delivered an ingredients box for each table. I gazed around the studio. Sunday and Jackson seemed really stoked. They had their hands on their ingredients box, and they were practically jumping up and down, eager to start.

On our other side, Ashli and Nathan stood calmly, gazing out at the cameras. They definitely were avoiding Nicole and me. Nathan still had a sick smirk on his face. Ashli fussed with her hair.

"Okay, chefs, open your ingredients box," Hess said. "Let's see what's for dinner."

I opened the lid and Nicole and I peered into the box. I saw a whole fish, silvery and plump. One eye stared up at us. I pulled out a box of rice, a bunch of carrots, and a bag of baking potatoes.

Nicole and I thought for a short while.

"We can make a fish soup," I said. "Soup with rice and carrots and potatoes."

Nicole frowned at the fish. "Think we can figure out how to fillet this thing? I've never deboned a fish."

"Neither have I," I said. "But we'd better not serve the judges fish bone soup."

That made us both laugh. Our first laugh since we came into the studio.

I lifted the fish carefully from the box and set it down on the counter. Nicole pulled out the rest of the ingredients.

We found a big soup pot in the cabinet. I filled it two-thirds full of water and set it on the stove to get it boiling.

Nicole found a knife in the counter drawer. We stood there for a moment, tapping the blade against the countertop, just studying the fish.

I raised my eyes and saw that Ashli and Nathan were already deboning their fish. Ashli slid the knife easily down the fish's side. Then she lifted the fish meat with one hand and simply tugged out the skeleton.

"Are you copying us?" Ashli shouted.

"If you don't know how to fillet a fish, Ashli and I could give you lessons after we win the contest," Nathan chimed in.

Hess stepped in front of our kitchen. "I love it when the chefs really put their hearts into it!" he exclaimed. He grinned at Ashli and Nathan. "You two really know how to wage a kitchen war!"

Nicole clenched her fists and did her angry tiger growl. She was breathing hard, her face twisted in anger.

"Just ignore them," I whispered to Nicole.

"Ignore them? How can we just ignore them?" she cried. "They're . . . they're . . . HORRIBLE JERKS!"

I pulled her to the counter. "Don't worry about them," I said softly. "It's our turn to take a little action."

She squinted at me. "What do you mean, Sascha?"

An evil smile crossed my face. "Let's see how they enjoy cooking up a batch of Monster Blood," I whispered.

23

I glanced at the tote bag I had hidden under the counter. I could picture the green gunk bubbling and churning inside it.

I had such an evil plan in mind. I almost burst out laughing. I leaned close and whispered it to Nicole.

Then we got down to business making our soup.

As I scraped the potatoes, I glanced over at Ashli and Nathan. They had a large casserole dish on their counter. Ashli had already peeled her potatoes. She was cutting them into thin slices. Nathan was shaking salt over the filleted fish.

On our other side, Sunday and Jackson had their fish spread out on a platter. Sunday was shaking a red spice over it. Probably paprika. Jackson was stirring a pot on the stove. I could see that it held the rice and chopped-up carrots.

The video cameras rolled in and out, recording us as we worked.

"Only fifteen minutes, chefs!" Hess boomed. "Better get cooking!"

Nicole poured the rice into the boiling water in our soup pot. "Now what?" she asked.

I motioned to our fish. "We have to remove its head," I said.

"Ewwwww." Nicole made a disgusted face and backed away. "Do you know how to do it?"

I shrugged. "I'm not sure," I said. "I think we have to *cut* it off. I don't think we can just *pull* it off."

I looked over to Ashli and Nathan. Maybe I could see how they removed their fish head.

But I was too late. Their fish head was already off. The fish had been cleaned beautifully, and the meat was sliced into neat sections.

I pulled a large chef's knife from the counter drawer. The biggest one I could find. "Let's just chop it off," I said.

Nicole shut her eyes. "I can't look."

I frowned at her. "Since when are you such a wimp?"

"Since I never cut a fish's head off!" she replied.

I raised the knife blade high. Nicole shut her eyes and spun away.

Slllaaaam.

I swung it down as hard as I could. The head made a soft *squisssh* sound and came off the body easily.

I let out a long sigh of relief. I wished the little

90

round black eye would stop staring at me. "It's okay to look," I told Nicole.

"Ten minutes!" Hess warned. "Chefs, your dish should be cooking by now."

Nicole and I finished chopping and slicing. We pulled the fish into small pieces. "Okay. We're ready," I said. "Everything into the soup pot."

Nicole nodded. She picked up the bowl of ingredients and carried it to the stove. Then she lifted the lid off the soup pot. I could hear the boiling water bubbling inside.

I picked up a towel and turned to wipe off the counter.

And that's when I heard Nicole's shriek.

"Oh, HELP ME!" she screamed. "OWWWW! Help me! I'm BURNED! Ohhhh, it HURTS! HELP! I'm BURNED!"

24

"CUT! CUT!" Hess's scream rose over Nicole's cries.

She stood gripping her right arm. The soup pot lid had fallen to the floor.

I stood frozen in place, staring straight ahead as crew members raced toward Nicole.

Ashli's eyes were wide with alarm. She dropped the potato peeler she had been using. She stepped around her counter and made her way into our kitchen. Nathan followed right behind her.

And that meant it was my turn to go into action.

Nicole had done an awesome job of pretending to be burned. Now I had to act quickly while everyone was huddling around her.

I moved along the counter while no one was watching me. Then I lifted the flap on the tote bag on the floor. I dug my hand deep inside—and broke off a nice chunk of Monster Blood.

It felt warm and wet and rubbery in my hand.

Behind me, Nicole was putting on a good show, wailing in pain.

"Can you move the fingers?" someone asked her. "Can you bend your wrist?"

"It doesn't look too red," I heard Hess say. "Maybe you were mostly startled."

"Should we call an EMT?" an assistant demanded.

I moved quickly. I slid into Ashli and Nathan's kitchen and darted to their casserole dish. I lifted the lid on it—and dumped the chunk of Monster Blood inside.

I set the lid back on the dish. Then I glanced all around, making sure no one saw me. I slipped back into our kitchen just as the group around Nicole was moving out.

"I . . . I think I'm okay," Nicole stammered. "I just got scared. But my hand is fine. Really."

Hess turned to his assistants. "Let's reset. Start again with ten minutes to go."

The crew members took their places. The camera operators moved behind their cameras. The three judges stopped their conversation and straightened up behind their table.

"Ten minutes, everyone," Hess announced. "Quiet on the set."

Nicole and I had our eyes on Nathan. He walked over to the casserole dish, lifted it, and put it in the oven.

Nicole grinned at me. "Now what? What's going to happen?"

25

The judging started, and Sunday and Jackson went first.

"It's a fish chowder," Sunday explained as their dish was poured into three bowls. "We used cream and a clear broth, plus the ingredients from the box."

They both glanced at Nicole and me. "It may not be hot enough," Jackson said. "Because of the interruption."

The judges muttered to one another. "It's hot enough," Jake said. "The temperature is fine. I'm a little disappointed in the flavor. You might have used more cream, I think."

Mary swallowed a mouthful of the chowder and licked her lips. "The flavor is okay, I think. But the potatoes are hard. Undercooked."

Next to her, Larry shrugged. "The dish is okay. Just okay," he said.

The assistants took away the chowder bowls.

Then they carried our soup pot to the judges' table and ladled out bowls of our fish soup.

I watched as the three judges sampled a few spoonfuls. I still wanted to win the contest. But I didn't feel the same excitement. I wasn't going to be upset if our soup didn't score big.

Mainly, I wanted to see what happened when the judges ate the Monster Blood. I know it was sick. But I think I cared more about my revenge plan than I did about winning.

"The soup is a little thin," Mary said. She took another taste. "Yes. A nice combination, and the ingredients are well cooked. But a little thin, Sascha and Nicole."

"I agree," Jake said, setting down his spoon. "It definitely could use more seasoning."

Wait till you taste Nathan and Ashli's dish, I thought. *It definitely has plenty of seasoning!*

The soup bowls were taken away, and Ashli and Nathan's casserole dish was carried to the judges' table. The judges helped themselves to big portions.

"Chef Ashli and Chef Nathan won the first round of our contest," Hess said into the camera. "Let's see if they can win round two. It's worth ten more points."

The three judges lowered their forks to their plates and began to sample the casserole. Nicole and I stood tensely. We both gripped the countertop and held our breath.

Jake licked his lips. "What is that unusual spice?" he asked.

"Very interesting and different," Mary said. She took a few more forkfuls. "I'm enjoying this. So many different flavors."

Nicole and I were afraid to look at each other. We kept our eyes straight ahead on the judges' table.

Larry held his fork up in front of him with a chunk of casserole on it. He studied it for a long moment. "I don't think I've ever tasted anything like it," he said.

Next to us, Ashli and Nathan were celebrating, pumping their fists above their heads.

I stared at the three judges as they helped themselves to more.

Come on, Monster Blood! I thought. *Come on! Do your thing!*

They had swallowed a lot of Monster Blood.

What was it going to do to them?

26

Nothing.

The Monster Blood did nothing.

The judges swallowed their last bite and wiped their mouths with their napkins. And they declared Ashli and Nathan the winners of the dinner round.

Come on, Monster Blood. Come on!

I didn't give up. I ignored Ashli and Nathan, who were fist-bumping each other and celebrating their victory. And I kept my eyes on the judges.

Nicole sighed. "It didn't work. We're losers," she murmured.

"We still have the dessert round," I said. "It's worth twenty points. We can still get a tie score, beat them in the tiebreaker, and win it all."

But I didn't believe that, and neither did she.

"Cut! Let's stop right there, everyone!" Hess shouted. "That's a wrap for today."

Ashli and Nathan continued to congratulate

each other. Sunday and Jackson looked as glum as Nicole and me.

"We will record the dessert round tomorrow," Hess announced. "Be here promptly at noon, chefs." He smiled at Ashli and Nathan. "They are cooking up a storm," he said. "But they can still be beat, everyone. You can still surprise them. Tomorrow will decide the winner of the Silver Spatula."

I watched the three judges walk out of the studio. They were laughing about something. They appeared to be in a good mood.

That wasn't right. They were supposed to be sick or something. The Monster Blood was supposed to make Ashli and Nathan's dish taste terrible. Or maybe do something to the judges so that Ashli and Nathan would lose big-time.

But Nicole and I knew who the big-time losers were. We were.

We walked home with our heads down. Clouds covered the late-afternoon sky. The houses, the trees, everything was in shades of gray. Perfect for my mood.

We crossed the street onto Nicole's block. Two little boys rocketed past us on their scooters. "That looks like fun," I muttered.

"Fun? What's fun?" Nicole replied glumly. She groaned as she shifted her backpack on her shoulders.

"At least I have an excuse to miss Toby's birth-day party tomorrow," I said.

Nicole shook her head. "It sounds like a night-mare. All those eight- and nine-year-olds in one room?"

"Yeah. A nightmare," I said. "I couldn't decide whether to go to Toby's birthday party or have all my teeth drilled."

Nicole laughed.

Then her eyes went wide. She stopped walking and grabbed my arm. "What's wrong?" I said.

"We forgot the Monster Blood, Sascha. We left it in the tote bag at the TV studio."

I gasped. "Oh, wow."

Nicole stared hard at me. "Think we should go back for it?"

I thought for a moment. "No," I said. "We don't have to go back there. The tote bag is tightly closed. It will be okay."

Boy, did I get THAT wrong!

27

"You and Nicole are wizards in the kitchen," Mom said at dinner. "I can't believe that other kids are better chefs than you."

"I have to admit Ashli and Nathan are pretty good cooks," I said. "And . . . they cheat."

Toby laughed. "You're a cheater, too. You always cheat when we play Uno."

He took a big bite of his hamburger and chewed with his mouth open. He sits across from me, and he knows that makes me sick.

"I don't have to cheat at Uno," I said. "You're such a loser player. I can win with a blindfold on."

"You cheated at breakfast," Toby said. "You took the last toaster waffle. And it was mine."

"Did it have your name on it?" I shot back. "I didn't see your name on it."

Mom gazed across the table at Dad. "Frank," she said. "Do you have anything to say about this?"

Dad blinked. "About what? Sorry. I wasn't listening. I was thinking about something else."

"Sascha was telling us how she and Nicole are losing on the TV cooking show," Mom said. "What were *you* thinking about?"

"Helium balloons," Dad answered. "I'm thinking we shouldn't get the helium balloons for Toby's party tomorrow."

Toby slammed both fists on the table. "Why not?" he demanded.

"Well . . . I'm imagining what you and your friends will do with the balloons," Dad said. "You'll pull them down and inhale the helium so you'll have funny voices."

"We will not!" Toby cried. But he couldn't keep a straight face. He burst out laughing. "They did that at Eden Franklin's party."

Mom turned to Toby. "Where were her parents?"

"Did you know there's a helium shortage in the world?" Dad said. "Maybe that's a good reason—"

"No!" Toby shouted. He tossed a carrot slice at Dad. "No! I want balloons! It's my party, and I want balloons!"

I stood up. "I'm done," I said. "Is it okay if I go up to my room?"

I could still hear them arguing about balloons from upstairs. I hurried into my room and shut the door.

I thought about doing some homework. But it was Friday night. Who does homework on a Friday night?

I sprawled on my bed. Took out my phone and watched some funny videos. Then I texted a few friends about what they were doing this weekend.

I was lying there staring at the ceiling when my door swung open and Toby burst in. "Hey, Sascha!"

"Who won the helium balloon fight?" I asked.

He tapped his thumb on his chest. "I did, of course."

I sat up. "Toby, why are you here? I told you a thousand times to knock before you come barging in."

"Give me back my birthday present," he said. "I want it back."

"You can't have it," I said. "I told you, I'm getting you another present."

He crossed his arms in front of him and stuck out his chin. "No. I want the Monster Blood. I want to show it to everyone at my party tomorrow."

"Just forget about it," I said. "It's too sticky and too creepy and—"

"But it's MINE!" He grabbed my arms and tried to tug me up from the bed. "It's MINE, Sascha. I want it back!"

"Toby, let go of me!" I pulled my arms free. It wasn't easy. He's stronger than he looks. Especially when he wants his way.

"Listen to me," I said. "I can't give the Monster Blood back to you. I returned it to the store."

Okay, I know. That was a lie.

But it was close to the truth. And believe me, it wasn't the *first* lie I had ever told him.

He stared into my eyes, studying me. Trying to figure out if I was telling the truth. "You took my present back? Really?"

I nodded. "It was just too sticky and dangerous. And it was *growing*."

He made a disgusted face at me. "Okay. Then you can't come to my party tomorrow. You are banished."

"Oooh. Big word," I said. "Where'd you learn that?"

"In a video game," he said. "But I mean it, Sascha. You're not invited."

I shrugged. "I can't come anyway, Toby. I have to go to the TV cooking show."

"You're going to LOSE!" he said. He punched me on the shoulder, spun around, and stomped out of the room.

What an animal. He really is a spoiled little criminal. But try telling that to Mom and Dad.

As soon as he was gone, my phone made a dinging noise. A text message.

I raised it to my face and read it. The text was from Nicole.

Please come over. I know it's late. But I'm really scared.

I texted her back: *Scared? Scared of what?*
Just come. Please.

28

"I know it's nine o'clock," I told Mom and Dad. "But it's not a school night. Tomorrow is Saturday."

"Sascha, it's a little late—" Dad started.

"I know. But I'm just going to run to Nicole's and then hurry right back. I'll be home in half an hour. I promise."

They exchanged glances. "Okay, but bring your phone," Mom said. "Call us if you want us to come pick you up."

"Mom, Nicole is only three blocks away. What could happen?" I said.

Yes. What could happen? What WAS happening? Why did Nicole say she was afraid?

I ran all the way to her house. It was a dark, moonless night. The air was heavy and wet, as if it was about to start raining again. And strong gusts of wind whistled and howled through the trees, making the branches creak and groan.

I was trying to straighten my windblown hair when Mrs. Hilliard opened the front door to their house. She blinked in surprise. "Sascha? Nicole didn't tell me you were coming."

Sparky, Nicole's little white dog, came hurrying to the front door, yapping excitedly. He jumped on me, front paws reaching my knees, short, stubby tail wagging like crazy.

Sparky and I are pals. I picked him up and hugged him.

Nicole's mom stepped aside so I could walk in. Their house was always warm and always smelled of coffee. I think Nicole's parents drank it all day long.

Sparky licked my face. I set him down, and he scampered away.

"I came to talk about the TV cooking show," I told her.

Another lie. It seemed to be a big night for lies.

"That's so exciting. You and Nicole on TV," she said, smiling.

"Well . . . yes," I replied. "I just wish—"

Nicole strode into the room before I could finish my sentence. "Hi, Sascha. Thanks for hurrying over."

"Nicole says you're having a little bad luck on the show," Mrs. Hilliard said. "But you're still in it, right? You can still win?"

I nodded. "Still in it."

Nicole stepped between me and her mother. "Sascha and I have to talk, Mom. It's important."

Mrs. Hilliard's mouth dropped open. "Well,

excuuuuse me." She pretended to be insulted. "Nice to see you, Sascha. Good luck tomorrow." Then she turned and walked toward the back of the house.

"What is it?" I whispered to Nicole. "Why are you scared?"

Nicole waited till her mom was completely gone. "We did the wrong thing," she whispered.

I dropped down on the ottoman in front of a brown leather armchair. "Huh? What are you talking about?"

Nicole sat on the edge of the couch across from me and leaned close so she could whisper. "We shouldn't have left the Monster Blood in the TV studio," she said.

She glanced behind her to make sure her mother hadn't returned. "What if it grows and grows and oozes out of the tote bag?"

"I already told you—" I started.

But she interrupted, her eyes wide with fear. "That tote bag has my name on it. If the Monster Blood gets out and destroys the studio and does horrible damage, they'll know who to blame."

"But, Nicole," I said, "the tote bag is closed up tight. And look what time it is. Almost ten o'clock. There won't be anyone there to let us in."

"We have to try," Nicole said, clasping her hands tensely in front of her. We have to get the Monster Blood back. I . . . I won't be able to sleep unless we do, Sascha."

106

I stood up. I could see she was seriously frightened. All kinds of thoughts spun around in my mind. I glanced out the window. Such a dark night. And so late . . .

"Nicole, the studio will be locked up tight," I said. "There's no way we'll get in."

"We have to try," she said. "We'll find a way, Sascha."

"But—" I started to argue with her some more. But I could see she would not give up.

"Okay, let's say we go," I said. "And somehow we get into the studio. Then what? What do we do with the stuff once we get it?"

Nicole shrugged. "I don't know. Dump it in a trash can, I guess." She stood up across from me. Her eyes locked on mine. "I only know I won't be able to sleep at all until I know the Monster Blood is out of the TV studio."

I stared back at her for a long moment.

"Okay," I said. "Let's go."

29

"We have to sneak out and hope my parents don't notice I'm gone," Nicole whispered. "They'll never let me go out this late."

Her parents were in the back, so we headed to the front door. Sparky followed right behind, wagging his tail. He thought he was going, too.

"Sorry, Sparky," Nicole said softly. "Not tonight."

The dog lowered his head, as if he understood.

I pulled open the front door, and a strong gust of wind almost blew us back into the house. "I think it's going to rain again," I said. "Should we get rain ponchos or something?"

"Let's just go," Nicole replied, giving me a push. "Let's get this over with."

Leaning into the wind, we made our way down to the street. I heard thunder in the distance, and the streetlamps flickered.

We started to trot side by side. Above us, old

tree limbs creaked and groaned and appeared to be waving us back.

The TV studio was three blocks from Nicole's house. I kept gazing up at the black sky, hoping the rain would hold off. "Maybe we can throw the stuff down a sewer," I said. "Or find a dumpster we can toss it in."

Nicole slipped on the wet grass but caught her balance. "We could leave the tote bag in front of the toy store," she said.

"If we could only find the toy store," I said, then pointed. "I could swear it was on that corner."

Nicole shook her head. "So weird. How could it just disappear?"

I wiped some raindrops off my forehead. The only other sounds were the cracking of tree branches and the *thud* of our shoes on the ground as we jogged.

The TV studio building came into view on the next block. Thin lines of lightning crackled high in the sky. A low explosion of thunder nearby made me jump.

"Hope we can find a way in," I said, my voice muffled by the thunder. I slowed down and pressed a hand against my throbbing side.

We both stopped in front of the entrance, struggling to catch our breath. A chill rolled down my back. I wiped sweat off my forehead with the sleeve of my jacket.

The big front window was completely dark. I tried the front door.

Locked.

I pulled it, then pushed it. But it wouldn't budge.

"Locked," I said. "I told you. Can we go home now?"

"Ring the bell," Nicole said. She pointed to an intercom on the wall beside the door. "Maybe there's a night security guard or something."

I hesitated. "If there's a security guard, what do we tell him?"

Nicole shrugged. "That we forgot something in the studio. That's all."

I pressed a few buttons on the intercom. We waited. No one came to the door.

I pressed them again. "No one here," I murmured. "Let's go home."

Nicole shivered. "Stop giving up. Maybe there's another door."

The rain pattered down a little harder. We ducked our heads and made our way around the side of the building.

We both stopped when we saw the half-open window. It was about shoulder high. A window shade flapped inside, tossed by the wind.

"I don't believe it," I said. "An open window. Okay. Maybe we can do this. Give me a boost. Then I'll pull you in."

I scraped both arms against the bricks reaching

110

for the windowsill. Nicole held me up while I pushed the window open higher. Then she boosted me, and I slid headfirst into the building.

A few seconds later, Nicole and I stood in the hallway outside the studio. A fuzzy yellow light glowed in the studio. And through the glass entrance doors, we could see the three kitchen areas and the judges' table. The video cameras were tilted down, as if sleeping.

I pressed my face against the glass and peered into the dim light. "I don't see any Monster Blood, Nicole," I said. "I think we're okay. It didn't get out of the bag."

"Let's make sure," she said. She pushed open one of the studio doors.

"Wait!" I grabbed her shoulder and held her back.

"What's wrong?"

"I thought I heard something," I whispered. "Footsteps maybe."

She gasped. We both froze. And listened.

My heart pounded so loud, I couldn't hear anything else.

Silence.

"False alarm," I said.

I followed her into the studio. Some of the food smells from the show lingered. The air felt warm and dry. The clock on the wall read 10:40.

I glanced around the floor. No sign of green gunk oozing anywhere. "The Monster Blood didn't get out," I told Nicole. "You can relax."

"Well, we're here," she said. "We have to take it and dump it somewhere."

I led the way to our kitchen space. Everything appeared just as we'd left it.

I'd stuffed the tote bag with the Monster Blood under the kitchen counter. We both leaned down to get it.

I gasped. My mouth dropped open.

"It's GONE!" Nicole cried.

30

"N-no way!" I stammered. I squinted in the dim light. I ducked under the counter and searched all around.

"Gone," Nicole said. "How can this *be*?"

"I know!" I said. "The cleaning crew. They must have come in to clean. And maybe they threw it out."

Nicole squinted at me. "Do you *think*?"

I frowned. "It's possible. That stuff couldn't walk out by itself. Besides, the tote bag was shut tight."

"You're wrong, Sascha. That's not what happened. The cleaners wouldn't throw out a perfectly good tote bag."

I sighed. "Maybe you're right."

Nicole grabbed my wrist. "What if Ashli and Nathan took it?"

"They couldn't," I said. "They left the studio before we did. The tote bag was here when we left."

Nicole locked her eyes on mine. "Well . . . what are we going to do?"

I shrugged. "Wait till tomorrow, I guess."

It took me hours to get to sleep. It was Nicole's fault. Every time I shut my eyes, I'd see that bubbling green goo oozing out of the tote bag and rising up like a living monster to the ceiling of the TV studio.

I finally had a few hours' sleep. I woke up late. It was almost eleven thirty. I heard voices and laughter and squealing downstairs. It took me a short while to realize that Toby's birthday party was already under way.

I squinted at the clock on my bed table and groaned. I had less than an hour to eat something, get dressed, and get to the TV studio.

I rushed into the bathroom to brush my teeth. I squeezed the toothpaste onto my toothbrush—and stopped. Dad had bought me *green* toothpaste! Did it remind me of Monster Blood? Three guesses.

Oh, wow. As I stared at it in horror, it began to bubble and bounce.

No. No way. Just my imagination.

I dropped the toothbrush into the sink and brushed my hair instead.

I heard a crash and then screams downstairs at the party. My brother began yelling, "Get off

114

me! Get *off* me!" And I guessed the party was off to a lively start.

I was so glad I was going to miss it.

I grabbed a protein bar for breakfast. Waved to my parents, who were opening pizza boxes in the dining room while ten eight- and nine-year-olds were practicing karate moves on one another in the den. And I trotted to the door, ready to make my escape.

As I reached for the doorknob, Toby jumped in front of me. He had chocolate smeared on his chin. I hoped he hadn't sampled the icing on his birthday cake already.

A sly grin spread above the chocolate. "Sascha, I have a secret," he said.

I rubbed a hand through his hair. "Happy birthday, fella," I said. (I *do* like the kid, after all.) "Have an awesome party. I'm outta here."

He brushed my hand off his head. "I have a secret, and I'm not telling you," he said.

I brought my face down close to his. "What's your secret?" I whispered.

"I'm not telling. I *told* you. It's a secret."

"Well, thanks for telling me," I said. "Aren't you even going to give me a hint?"

But he spun away and ran back to his screaming, laughing friends.

I stepped outside and closed the front door behind me. The silence felt so good!

I walked to the studio and waved to Nicole as I stepped through the glass doors. "You beat me here," I said as I entered our kitchen. "I had to make my way through an obstacle course—Toby's party."

Nicole motioned to the judges' table with her head. "Something going on over there," she said. "Some kind of problem."

I turned and saw the three judges huddled behind their table. Larry was scratching his head and frowning. Mary and Jake were both talking at once.

The crew had grown silent. Everyone was turned toward the judges.

Hess lifted one of their wooden chairs off the floor and examined it. He set it back on the floor and motioned for Larry to sit down in it.

I let out a sharp cry as I saw what the problem was.

Larry was too large. The judges had all grown too large.

They didn't fit in their chairs!

31

Major panic. Everyone started shouting and talking at once.

All three judges were yelling at Hess. Courtney and Morgan, the two assistants, hurried over and quickly got into the shouting match.

"Is this some kind of practical joke?" Larry cried. He had to be at least seven feet tall now. "Did you bring out smaller chairs to make us look stupid?"

"This is ridiculous!" Jake picked up his chair and heaved it across the studio.

"I don't understand this," Mary said, scowling at Hess. Her face darkened to red. "I was perfectly normal when I drove over here. Am I really bigger? How did this happen?"

Beside us, Sunday and Jackson stared in disbelief. Ashli and Nathan stepped out of their kitchen and began snapping photos with their phones.

Crew members pointed, shaking their heads, wide-eyed.

Nicole and I stood watching the whole scene with our mouths hanging open. We were the only two people in the room who knew the truth. The only ones who knew why the judges had started bulging and stretching.

The Monster Blood they had eaten took its time. But it was making them grow now.

"It . . . it's all our fault," Nicole stammered.

I swallowed. My mouth was suddenly dry as cotton. "Maybe they won't find out," I whispered.

"But look what we did to them!" Nicole exclaimed. "If they *do* find out it was our fault . . ." Her voice trailed off.

I felt sick. Had we really ruined the judges' lives?

"We have to finish!" Hess was screaming. "We have no choice. We have to finish the show today!"

"No way!" Mary screamed. "I can't go on TV looking like this! I'm eight feet tall and I'm bursting out of my dress."

"Look at me!" Jake cried. "I . . . I can't believe this. My clothes are *ripping*! They don't fit at all!"

"People? People?" the deep voice on the loudspeaker broke in. "People? Can we have quiet, please?"

Everyone kept shouting, heads shaking, hands flying in the air.

"I'm sure we can figure this out," the voice said. "But we need quiet."

118

"It's not our fault!" Hess screamed. "I don't know how this happened to you three. But it isn't our fault. We do not have a stretching machine to make our judges suddenly bigger!"

"Haha. Funny," Jake snapped sarcastically. "Do you think this is a joke? You won't think it's funny when we all sue you!"

"People, people . . ." The voice on the loud-speaker returned. "We can talk about all this later. We only have the studio for two hours. We must finish the show. Then—"

"How can you finish the show?" Jake cried. "We have to see doctors. We have to be examined. Something gave us these growth spurts. Are we going to keep growing and growing?"

"Was it something we ate here?" Mary demanded.

My whole body shuddered. *Nicole and I . . . We're going to get caught. Our parents will be sued. Our lives are ruined!*

"Wait! Hold on, everyone!" Hess cried, waving his hands above his head. "Everyone—listen. I have an idea."

It took a while to get everyone quiet. Then Hess frantically pointed to the wall across the studio. "In the supply closet . . . ," he said. "We have bigger chairs . . . in that closet over there."

"So what?" Jake demanded.

All three judges were glaring angrily at Hess.

"We'll put you in the bigger chairs," Hess told

them. "And you'll look normal. We can finish the show and—"

"But we're not normal!" Mary cried.

Hess raised both hands in front of him. "I know. I know. But let's just finish the show in the bigger chairs. And then we'll get you the help you need. I promise."

He didn't wait for an answer. He turned to his two assistants and told them to bring the bigger chairs from the closet.

They hurried across the studio.

Pulled open the closet door.

My scream of horror echoed off the studio ceiling. I screamed so loud, I started to choke. Shrill shrieks and terrified cries rang out all around.

An ENORMOUS blob of Monster Blood exploded from the closet. Bigger and taller than a bear, glowing in the bright lights, it rolled over the two assistants. Their squeals were cut short. They didn't stand a chance. It was like they were swallowed up.

32

Nicole and I huddled against each other behind our counter as the monstrous ball of gunk bounced over the floor. We could see Morgan and Courtney glued to one side, struggling and squirming, unable to unstick themselves.

"It . . . it's gigantic!" I cried.

"Who put it in that closet?" Nicole asked in a trembling voice. "The cleaning crew?"

I shrugged. "Beats me."

"I *knew* we needed to get it last night," Nicole said, shaking her head. "Now . . . it's too late."

The enormous ball of Monster Blood rolled over one of the camera guys. He uttered a scream as he stuck to its slimy, shimmering surface.

And then, as if alive, the Monster Blood took a big bounce. It sailed over the judges' table—and swallowed all three judges.

I covered my ears to try to block out the roar of screams all around me. My heart beat so hard, I thought I might explode.

I held on to Nicole's hand as the big, quivering ball rolled across the studio floor. Six people rolled with it, bouncing on it, screaming their heads off, and squirming, twisting to free themselves.

Hess dodged to one side as the blob came rolling toward him. He landed on the floor, and the Monster Blood rolled over him. Trapping him, too.

"Nicole—why are we standing here?" I cried.

Most everyone had run from the studio.

"Let's go!" I gave her a hard tug. She seemed frozen, unable to move.

"Wh-what are we going to do?" she stammered. Her whole body trembled.

"We're going to RUN!" I said. I pulled her again, and we took off.

We joined the frantic stampede out the glass doors and down the long hall. We were almost outside when someone screamed, "*It's coming after us!*"

Nicole and I bolted through the front door. We didn't slow down. We kept running along the small patch of grass in front of the building.

When I turned around, I saw Ashli and Nathan stuck to the Monster Blood. It swept over the grass like a giant tidal wave—a tsunami of green gunk. Carrying its screaming, twisting prisoners.

I stopped and watched. It was like a horror movie come to life.

And it was all my fault. All my brilliant idea.

That thought made it almost impossible for me to move.

But then I had *another* thought.

"Run, Sascha! Keep going!" Nicole cried. She reached out to pull me across the street. But I swung away from her.

"Run! Why aren't you running?" she cried. "It's going to swallow us, too!"

I grabbed her by the shoulders and stopped her. "Wait," I said. "Stop running. Hold on. I think I know what's going on here. I think I know how to stop it."

33

Nicole tugged me again. "Let's go!"

"No. Wait." I pulled back.

I wanted to cover my ears from the screams of terror behind us. I saw the huge blob of Monster Blood bounce over more people, trapping them against it.

"We don't need to run," I told Nicole. "This isn't really happening."

She gasped. "Huh? Not happening? Are you okay?"

"Listen to me," I said. "It's all a nightmare I'm having."

Nicole squinted at me. I could see I was totally confusing her.

I grabbed her shoulders. "Remember when that car roared around the corner and knocked me to the sidewalk?"

She nodded. "Yes. But—"

"I hit my head, remember," I continued.

More shrill screams behind us, coming closer.

"It must have knocked me out, Nicole," I said. "Don't you see? This isn't real. You're not really here. We're not having this conversation."

I squeezed her shoulders tighter. "This is all a dream I'm having. A terrible nightmare."

She pulled away from me. "Sascha, let's talk about it later. Let's run now!"

"No. We don't have to run. All I have to do is wake myself up."

"Let's wake you up later," she demanded, her voice trembling with fear. "Let's get away from this thing and *then* wake up."

"But it's not real, Nicole," I said. "I just have to pull myself out of this nightmare—and everything will be fine again."

Her whole body shuddered. Screams rang out as the Monster Blood bounced and rolled, carrying its victims.

Okay. I'm going to try this. I'm going to end this nightmare. I gritted my teeth hard and shut my eyes tight.

Wake up, Sascha, I told myself. *Wake up. Come on—wake up!*

34

Was it happening? Was I waking myself up?

I opened my eyes. I blinked several times. "I'm awake," I whispered.

But then I saw Nicole's terrified face. And the gigantic tidal wave of Monster Blood rolling toward us, so fast . . . so fast.

It shimmered in the afternoon light. And the thrashing arms and legs of the people stuck to its surface made it look like a humongous insect, swallowing everything in its path.

I uttered a sigh. My legs trembled. I thought I might collapse to the ground. "It . . . didn't work," I murmured. "It isn't a dream."

We didn't say another word. We spun to the street and took off running. We ran through a vacant lot and, breathing hard, started to cross someone's front yard.

I glanced behind us to see if the monstrous gunk was following us—and tripped over something. A rake on the lawn.

Pain raced up my body. I struggled to get back to my feet.

Too late.

Too late!

The sky appeared to darken to green. Like a floating green cloud, it swept over Nicole and me.

I made a loud *thunnnk* sound as my back stuck to the gooey surface. I uttered a terrified cry and struggled to keep my head out where I could breathe.

Nicole and I both stuck to the wall of Monster Blood. I squirmed and pulled and tried to heave myself free. But I wasn't strong enough.

"It's got us!" Nicole cried, beside me. "It's . . . sucking us inside!"

35

I could feel the pulsing force of the Monster Blood as it pulled me deeper into the green goo. I slapped at it with both hands. But my back was stuck tight against it. As it pulled me in, the bubbling sound almost drowned out the screams and cries of the other prisoners.

I turned and saw Hess's head poking out from inside the green wall. The rest of his body had disappeared inside the gunk.

My hands disappeared inside the goo. I was helpless now. I glanced around—and saw Ashli and Nathan staring back at me *from INSIDE the Monster Blood!*

I turned to Nicole. Her eyes were wide with terror. Large teardrops rolled down her cheeks. The ball of Monster Blood bounced, and she disappeared inside it.

"S-sorry, Nicole," I stammered. "I'm so sorry."

And then over the screams and the bubbling of the Monster Blood, I heard another sound.

A low roar.

Like beats of distant thunder.

A pounding noise. Like boots thudding against the ground.

With a hard tug, I pulled my head away from the goo and turned my eyes toward the approaching sounds. "Huh?" I uttered a gasp.

And stared at a group of *giants*. Hurrying toward us. A bunch of giant *boys*?

They had to be thirty feet tall! They were trotting fast, swinging their arms as they ran. Boys as tall as trees . . . And wait!

That boy's face! Was it Toby? A giant Toby leading the pack?

Now I really AM dreaming! I told myself. *This can't be happening!*

But yes, I was staring in shock at a giant Toby. And I recognized some of his friends. Kids he had invited to his birthday party. Only huge. I had to tilt my head and gaze up into the sun to see their faces.

The other prisoners grew silent as the giants came near.

"Hey, Toby—!" I tried to shout to him. But in my terror, no sound came out of my mouth.

I wanted to wave. But my hands were stuck to the side of the pulsing Monster Blood.

"Toby! What happened to you? What are you doing?" That's what I wanted to shout. But now my voice came out in a choked whisper.

And then Toby and his friends were standing in front of the wall of green goo. And they were as tall as the goo.

"Sascha!" Toby's voice boomed, so loud my name rang in my ears.

He grabbed me around the waist with his enormous hands. And yanked me from the sticky gunk.

He spun me away from the Monster Blood and set me down on the ground. And then Toby turned and began ripping away at the green wall.

I sat on the ground, struggling to catch my breath. And I watched Toby's friends—the other giant boys—frantically rip and tear at the Monster Blood. They pulled off big chunks and tossed them to the ground.

Giant Toby hoisted Nicole into the air and set her down beside me. She sat blinking and shaking her head. Droplets of Monster Blood clung to her hair.

I saw Ashli and Nathan staggering away. Hess escaped and went running back toward the TV studio.

Toby and his giant friends shouted and cheered as they ripped the wall of Monster Blood to shreds. Big chunks of it shimmered dully on the grass.

It didn't take long for everyone to escape. Toby and his giant friends tossed the last shreds of the gooey green gunk to the ground.

Then they formed a circle around Nicole and me. We climbed to our feet, still breathing hard.

"Are you both okay?" Toby asked. His voice boomed down at us.

"T-Toby," I stammered. "What happened? How did you do this?"

He grinned. "Remember? When you left the house? I told you I had a secret."

I blinked. "Secret? What secret?"

"The second can of Monster Blood," he answered. "I think you forgot about it, Sascha."

The second can? Yes. I did forget.

I bought two cans. I left the second one in my closet.

Toby's grin grew wider. "I found the second can, and guess what? I brought it downstairs to my party."

"Toby, you didn't—" Nicole started.

He nodded. "Yes, I did. I passed the can around and we all ate some. It was awesome!"

"But look at you!" I cried. "You're all *giants*!"

"No problem," he boomed, leaning over me. "I read the small print on the can."

He motioned to his friends. They turned away from us and spread out over the grass. Then they began stomping the ground with their gigantic feet.

Thud. Thuddd. Thuddddd.

Nicole and I watched as the boys stomped on the chunks of Monster Blood. Smashed them. Crushed them.

I grabbed Nicole's shoulder. "Look—the pieces of Monster Blood are shrinking!"

Thud thud thuddd.

Yes, as the boys stomped on them, the green chunks were shrinking. And as Nicole and I watched in amazement, the boys shrank, too.

"Ta-daa!" Toby raised his fists over his head in triumph. "We're all back to normal!" Everyone cheered and fist-bumped.

"What do we do now?" Toby asked.

"Go home!" I exclaimed.

Nicole and I burst out laughing, just from being so happy the whole thing was over. We turned and started to follow Toby and his friends.

But we stopped when we saw a man running toward us, frantically waving his arms.

Heston Hill. "Hey—! Hey—!" he shouted to us, gripping his phone in one hand. He stopped and took a few seconds to catch his breath.

"I—I—I got the whole thing on video!" he stammered, raising his phone in front of us. "Forget cooking! This is going to be the best *horror show* ever!"

36

I felt so happy. I kept clapping Nicole on the back and cheering. I felt as if I had won a war. I guess I actually had.

The Monster Blood was gone, and so were all my worries. I could breathe normally again. I could feel all my tension melting away.

I gazed up at the blue sky. So beautiful. So shiny and clear.

"Hey, wait—!" I uttered.

I stared up at the sky—and gasped when I suddenly realized I wasn't standing up. I was lying on my back.

Why am I here, stretched out on the ground?

My head throbbed. I twisted it to the right. I saw Nicole gazing at me, her eyes wet with tears, her face pale and tight.

And then I saw the ambulance. The two young men in light blue uniform shirts. Paramedics?

Paramedics? For me?

I shut my eyes against the pulsing pain of my headache.

When I opened them, Nicole was leaning over me.

"Wh-what is happening?" My voice came out in a choked whisper.

"Oh, I'm so happy!" Nicole gushed. "I'm so happy you're awake, Sascha."

"Huh?" I squinted up at her, not quite understanding.

"We were on our way to the TV studio," Nicole said, wiping a tear off her cheek. "But we never made it. That car . . . it came squealing around the corner and knocked you over. You hit your head, Sascha. You've been out cold ever since."

My mouth dropped open. I stared up at her. "Really? Really??"

EPILOGUE FROM SLAPPY

Hey, was it a dream or not?

If it was a dream, why is Nicole's hair still sticky with green goo?

And what's that gloppy green gunk bubbling under *your* bed?

Don't *stick* around. Better go check it out.

I'm going to get something to eat. That story made me hungry—hungry for more HORROR! Hahahaha.

Don't worry. I'll cook up another story for you when I return with another Goosebumps SlappyWorld book.

Remember, this is Slappy's world.

You only *scream* in it!

SLAPPYWORLD #14:
FIFTH-GRADE ZOMBIES

Read on for a preview!

Well, do you believe it?

Here I am, Todd Coates, a city kid my whole life, from Queens, New York. I'm bouncing on a bus through Wisconsin Dells, on a narrow bumpy country road. Watching the trees blur past. And the fields ... the dry, brown farm fields stretching toward who-knows-where.

Todd Coates. From the Greatest City on Earth. The Big Apple. On my way to living on a farm for a year. Is that possible?

The only farms I've ever seen were in the movies. They looked like living on Mars to me. I mean, where do the farm people go for good Thai food? And do they have Wi-Fi?

I'm not a nature guy. Maybe you've guessed that. Sure, I see trees when I'm rollerblading in the park. But I'm not sure I've ever even touched a tree.

I lie in my bed at night and listen to the garbage trucks out on the street. The whine and growl of garbage trucks are like a lullaby to a city kid like me. But farm life? I couldn't picture it.

Guess what? I had nightmares about the farm. I saw myself sleeping on a pile of hay with chickens pecking at my pajamas.

But don't get me started about nightmares.

Anyway, here I was, on this squeaky bus, on this county road, sunlight and shadows rolling across the windows. We passed the town of Baraboo, so I knew we were getting close. My cousins' farm is about twenty miles west of Baraboo. It's near a town called Moose Hollow, so small it's not even on the map. Believe that?

I don't mean to make fun. My Aunt Clara and Uncle Jake are great people. When my parents had to go off on their long business trip, they were the only ones in my family who could take me.

Aunt Clara said it would be an educational year for me.

She got that right!

I didn't know my cousins Mila and Skipper very well. But I was glad I wouldn't be the only kid on the farm. Mila is my age, 12. And Skipper is a few years older.

I FaceTimed with them a few times. Mila seemed nice. A little quiet and shy. Aunt Clara likes to gush. I mean, she's always rah-rah like a cheerleader. I think she could get excited over cornflakes in the morning.

Uncle Jake was the opposite. He kept scratching

his cheeks and clearing his throat and muttering away from the phone. I guess he doesn't like FaceTime.

And Skipper was weird, too. He's about a foot taller than everyone else in the family. He has a croaky voice, like it's still changing. And he seemed really tense. He kept blinking a lot and glancing around. I don't know what his problem was.

The second time I FaceTimed with Skipper, he slid his face up real close to the screen, and he whispered, "Todd, don't believe everything you hear."

How weird was that?

I mean, I hadn't heard *anything at all*.

Do you think he was trying to scare me?

The bus hit a hard bump, and I nearly went flying from my seat. It was late afternoon, and the shadows across the farm fields were stretching longer.

I pulled my phone from my jeans pocket and tried to call Mom and Dad back in New York. They were still home. They weren't leaving on their trip till the weekend.

But all I got was silence. No cell service way out here in the wilderness. I couldn't even send a text.

I slid the phone back into my pocket and pulled out my harmonica. My stomach was starting to feel fluttery. I could feel myself growing tense as we came closer to Moose Hollow. And one thing that always helped to calm me down was to blow a little blues on my harp.

It's not anything fancy. It's a Hohner Special 20 in the key of C. Sort of a beginner's harmonica. My parents bought it for me for my eleventh birthday.

I've spent so many hours practicing on it that I should be a lot better. But I don't care. Playing the instrument always makes me feel good.

I brought two special things with me to the farm. One was the harmonica. The other was a red plastic lighter. I never light the thing. I don't even know if it will flame anymore. My Grandpa Dave gave it to me a few days before he died. He carried it with him everywhere. Always in his pocket. Maybe he even slept with it. I don't know. I do know he thought it was special. So I've treasured it as a good-luck charm ever since.

I gripped my harmonica and squinted out the dusty bus window at the passing fields. What were those animals poking up from the dirt? They weren't squirrels, and they weren't rabbits.

Maybe I really *had* traveled to another planet!

I raised the harmonica to my mouth, slid it back and forth a few times—and started to play. I don't really play songs on it. I sort-of free-form it. I like to get a rhythm going and then improvise a melody.

I was pumping out some pretty good sounds when a shout made me stop. It was the bus driver up at the front. He was a red-faced old guy with a blue-and-white bandana tied around his bald head.

"Put that away, kid," he called. "Back in your pocket, okay?"

"I was playing softly," I said. I sat halfway to the back, so I had to shout.

About the Author

R.L. Stine says he gets to scare people all over the world. So far, his books have sold more than 400 million copies, making him one of the most popular children's authors in history. The Goosebumps series has more than 150 titles and has inspired a TV series and two motion pictures. R.L. himself is a character in the movies! He has also written the teen series Fear Street, and the Mostly Ghostly and Nightmare Room series. He is currently writing a series of graphic novels entitled Just Beyond. R.L. Stine lives in New York City with his wife, Jane, an editor and publisher. You can learn more about him at rlstine.com.

Catch the
MOST WANTED
Goosebumps® villains
UNDEAD OR ALIVE!

SPECIAL EDITIONS

REVENGE OF THE LIVING DUMMY
R.L. STINE

CREEP FROM THE DEEP
R.L. STINE

MONSTER BLOOD FOR BREAKFAST!
R.L. STINE

THE SCREAM OF THE HAUNTED MASK
R.L. STINE

DR. MANIAC VS. ROBBY SCHWART
R.L. STINE

WHO'S YOUR MUMMY?
R.L. STINE

MY FRIENDS CALL ME MONSTER
R.L. STINE

SAY CHEESE - AND DIE SCREAMING!
R.L. STINE

WELCOME TO CAMP SLITHER
R.L. STINE

The Original Bone-Chilling Series

—with Exclusive Author Interviews!

NIGHT of the LIVING DUMMY
R.L. STINE

DEEP TROUBLE
R.L. STINE

MONSTER BLOOD
R.L. STINE

the HAUNTED MASK
R.L. STINE

ONE DAY at HORRORLAND
R.L. STINE

the CURSE of the MUMMY'S TOMB
R.L. STINE

BE CAREFUL WHAT YOU WISH FOR
R.L. STINE

SAY CHEESE and DIE!
R.L. STINE

the HORROR at CAMP JELLYJAM
R.L. STINE

HOW I GOT MY SHRUNKEN HEAD
R.L. STINE

R. L. Stine's Fright Fest!
Now with Splat Stats and More!

GET YOUR HANDS ON THEM BEFORE THEY GET THEIR HANDS ON YOU!

CONTINUE THE FRIGHT
AT THE GOOSEBUMPS SITE
scholastic.com/goosebumps

FANS OF GOOSEBUMPS CAN:

- PLAY THE GHOULISH GAME: GOOSEBUMPS: SLAPPY'S DROP DEAD HOUSE

- LEARN ABOUT NEW BOOKS AND TERRIFYING CLASSICS

- TAKE A QUIZ AND LEARN WHICH TYPE OF MONSTER YOU ARE!

- LEARN ABOUT THE AUTHOR WHO STARTED IT ALL: R.L. STINE

THE *Goosebumps* SERIES COMES TO LIFE IN A BRAND-NEW DIGITAL WORLD

MEET Slappy—and explore the *Goosebumps* Zone.
PLAY games, create an avatar, and chat with other fans.

Start your adventure today! Download the **HOME BASE** app and scan this image to unlock exclusive rewards!

SCHOLASTIC.COM/HOMEBASE

Goosebumps

SlappyWorld

THIS IS SLAPPY'S WORLD—
YOU ONLY SCREAM IN IT!

■SCHOLASTIC